LINDA CRAMMOND

troika

Published by TROIKA

First published 2017

Troika Books Ltd

Well House, Green Lane, Ardleigh CO7 7PD, UK

www.troikabooks.com

A CIP catalogue record for this book is available

from the British Library

ISBN 978-1-909991-48-4

1 2 3 4 5 6 7 8 9 10

The horse half closed his eyes and relaxed his neck muscles under the smooth and steady strokes of the brush. His skin twitched with pleasure as the bristles scraped away the sweat and dust, leaving his coat glowing with health. The brush moved to his head, tracing careful circles round his eyes and gently kneading the ticklish bits round the base of his ears. Lovely. She knew just how he liked it and she was always gentle – even when she was acting fierce. But why didn't she ever take him out? He loved their games in the paddock but he missed the wide open spaces: the distant light on the marsh, the sting of salt in the air and the pounding of his hooves through the waves.

Chapter 1

It was the second worst Christmas Kiri had ever known. She wasn't going to think about the worst one – that would make her cry – but she didn't want to think about this one either, or she wouldn't be able to get through it. She'd woken at dawn in their ramshackle farmhouse on the Romney Marshes and looked instinctively for the stocking, which her mother had always hung at the end of her bed. Of course it wasn't there, and its absence closed round her heart with an icy grip.

Getting out of bed, she stubbed her toe on the wooden chest. The sudden pain wiped out the greater pain of missing her mother – but only for a few seconds. She climbed on to the window seat and stared over the marshes, which her mother had loved to paint. No white Christmas this year with hoar frost turning the long grass into swan's feathers, just a cold, grey sky to match her mood.

She pulled on her muckiest sweater and stable jeans and crept downstairs. Not that there was much danger of waking her father and his girlfriend. They always slept late at weekends. Stephanie Eland, a Londoner who'd been living in New York for years, was in the process of divorcing her American husband and moving back to Britain. But not, Kiri hoped, to Walland Farm. She let herself out of the back door and ran across the field to the tumbledown barn, which housed the stables. Her heart warmed for the first time that morning when she heard Foxfire give his special whinny. She grabbed a bucket of feed she'd left ready the night before and poured it into his manger.

'Happy Christmas, Foxy!' she said, tipping in the last of the horse pellets and brushing his forehead with her lips. Foxfire was a flaming red chestnut, a colour he'd inherited from a Portuguese Lusitano sire and a thoroughbred dam. He belonged to her elder brother but Kiri was looking after him while Eddie was on his gap year in New Zealand, staying with some distant cousins. For such a powerful horse, Foxy was a surprisingly dainty eater and she left him to nibble his way through breakfast while she took the other bucket to her old grey pony, Mouse.

'Christmas treat,' she said, putting the bucket under his nose and wrapping her arms round his neck. Mouse always filled her with happy memories – galloping on the beach, jumping cross-country or just messing about in the paddock. He'd taught her everything she knew about riding, but she'd outgrown him and he was too old to go on loan to another family, so he was living in honourable retirement in the paddock. He was allowed grass and hay but none of Foxy's high protein diet except on special days. The pony snorted in surprise and gulped the pellets down as if he hadn't eaten for months. He was her oldest friend and, since Eddie left, she felt as if he was the only creature in the world she could confide in.

'Happy Christmas!' she whispered in his ear. 'I'd like to spend the whole day with you and Foxy.' She rubbed his nose and sighed. 'If only. But I'll be stuck indoors all day on my best behaviour for *her*.' Even if the sun came out, Kiri was certain her father's girlfriend wouldn't leave the house. Steph's only concession to the countryside was wearing five-inch heels instead of six, and she wasn't going to risk her latest Jimmy Choos on real grass.

After making up feed and hay nets for the evening, Kiri turned Foxy out and started to walk reluctantly back to the house. She stopped when she heard him paw the ground and whinny. Not the welcoming whinny he gave her every morning but something shriller.

'You're bored,' she thought, 'just like me.' He flicked his tail in an invitation to play and trotted along the fence beside her. She stood still, screwing up her eyes while she made up her mind. Eddie had told her not to take Foxy out of the paddock.

'He's too much horse for you,' he'd said. 'He'll bolt and you'll both get hurt. Much better to school him loose in the paddock and carry on with the tricks. That'll keep his mind exercised as well as his body.' That was what she'd been doing until now. But it wasn't enough. Kiri missed riding across the marsh as much as Foxy did. Since she'd outgrown Mouse, she'd only had a few chance rides in return for doing odd jobs at the local riding stables. She kept hoping her father would get her another pony but he said two horses were already too many at Walland Farm. She longed to be riding, really riding, again.

Foxy snorted and the warm breath from his nostrils condensed in the cold air. Like dragon's breath, thought Kiri. And dragons needed to fly.

Yes! Adrenalin fired through her veins at the thought of galloping Foxy on the beach. She led him back to his stall in the barn, unlocked the lean-to that was used as a tack room and put on his saddle and bridle with trembling fingers. He was quivering with excitement too. Quickly, before she could change her mind, she fastened her riding helmet and swung herself into the saddle. His muscles tensed when she turned him on to the bridle path, which led to Camber Sands, and she barely touched his sides with her legs before he moved into a ground-covering trot. It was like floating on air. Her dark hair whipped out behind her, and when he leapt forward into a canter she gave a shout of pure happiness. She'd never been on such a powerful horse and his strength tempted her to go faster, but not yet.

'Steady,' she told him. 'Wait till we're on the sand.'

Soon, too soon, they were approaching the end of the bridle path where it crossed the main road and Kiri gave a tug on the reins. Foxfire took no notice. Again she pulled on the reins, harder this time, but he wouldn't stop or even slow. She heard herself choke back a sob of terror as she pictured a car speeding towards the intersection. Panic was rising in her throat like bile but she fought to control it. Horses could smell fear, and if Foxy sensed her terror it would only make him go faster. She took a deep breath, pushed her weight to the back of the saddle and gave a series of steady pulls against his mouth. At last he started to slow but it was too late. She screamed as he skidded across the road with hooves slithering on the tarmac, but luck was with them – there was no car, no thud of metal tearing into flesh.

Although Foxy was almost on his knees with Kiri halfway up his neck, he hauled himself up with a lurch that threw her back into the saddle. They plunged over the soft dunes at the top of the beach and hit the smooth, firm sand, which curved round the bay like a racecourse. Foxy snatched at the bit and surged into a flat-out gallop. For a moment, Kiri thought of fighting him, but the thrill of speed was infectious. She leant forward in the saddle and let him go, his hooves pummelling the wet sand and his chestnut mane flying in her face. She flung one arm high and gave a cry of elation, a cry echoed by a lone surfer at the edge of the water. For a second, their eyes met and they grinned – two crazy people doing what they loved on a deserted Christmas morning.

Long as the beach was, it was coming to an end, so Kiri steered Foxy towards the sea, hoping it would slow him down. It didn't. He plunged over the waves as if they were fences to be jumped, and she had to wrench him back towards the beach before they got caught in the rip tide. At last he slowed to a trot and then a walk. His breath rasped, and his flanks heaved under a coating of sweat and salt. The elation Kiri had felt only a moment ago was swamped by guilt. Eddie had been right: she'd taken them both into danger. She just prayed that Foxy wouldn't pay for her recklessness with ripped tendons or a strained heart.

Chapter 2

For over an hour after they got home, Kiri struggled to undo the damage she'd done. Foxy stood head down, shivering from the strain of the gallop as the sweat dried on his skin. First she dipped a sponge in warm water and sluiced off the caked sand and salt. Then she used a plastic scraper to squeeze the water out of his coat. A rug couldn't go straight on to wet skin, so she 'thatched' him by putting a thick layer of hay under the rug to start the drying process. Next came his delicate and precious legs, always a horse's most vulnerable points. She ran her hand anxiously down the tendons and wrapped them carefully in dry bandages. It was too soon to let him drink, so she wiped his mouth with a sponge and gave him a small hay net. He was still trembling. She didn't dare leave him alone to get clothes for herself from the house, so she towelled her hair with an old rag and pulled Mouse's spare rug round her own shivering shoulders.

'I'm sorry,' she told Foxy. 'I'll never, ever let that happen again.'

Two hours after they got home, Foxy took a first nibble of hay from the net. Kiri gave a sigh of relief: he was going to be all right. She gave him a half-bucket of water, a heartfelt kiss and walked shakily back to the house.

She opened the door to the kitchen and suppressed a groan at the smell of camomile tea. Steph was up. She was sitting at the table, her elegant, Armani-clad legs neatly crossed, and a grey silk shirt setting off her genuine Caribbean tan and cap of smooth blond hair. Kiri had never seen her perfect oval face without an hour's worth of immaculate make-up, and today was no exception.

'Darling,' said Steph, 'Merry Christmas.' She spoiled it by wrinkling her delicate nose. 'You do smell of stable.'

'Happy Christmas,' muttered Kiri, thinking it would be anything but with Steph in residence. She scuttled through the kitchen into the utility room where she stuffed the offending clothes in the washer. Padding upstairs in her shirt and pants, she noticed steam drifting out of the bathroom. She longed to soak in a hot bath but if Steph had indulged in one of her half-hour showers, their ancient hot water system would be on strike and she'd have to make do with a quick wash. She put on clean jeans and a red T-shirt stamped with a picture of a horse and the words 'I'd rather be jumping'. It was last year's present from Eddie. She hoped Steph would get the message.

After a quick visit to the stable to check on Foxy – he was still nibbling the hay – she found her father standing in front of the Christmas tree in the sitting room. He gave her a lung-crusher of a hug. Jim McFarlane was a short but forceful man with grey-green eyes and light brown hair. Eddie was just like him and not only in looks: he'd inherited the ambition and drive that had propelled their father out of a Liverpool slum to become owner of a successful property company. Kiri took after her mother's side of the family: tall, dark and slender – or in her case, beanpole skinny. She'd decided long ago that, although she'd inherited her mother's wide brown eyes, she'd missed out on her dreamy beauty. Looking at the Christmas tree and thinking of her mother made the tears start.

'I know it's hard,' said her father. 'But Mum would want us to remember the good times and not the bad.'

Kiri nodded, but the bad times were hard to forget. It was only two years ago to the day that her mother had finally given in to cancer. The black hole left by her death never seemed to get any smaller. Kiri loved her dad but he was often away and, now that Steph was on the scene, she found it hard to talk to him. The buzz of her father's phone broke into her thoughts.

'It's Edward.' Her father's face brightened. Her brother had got better-than-expected exam results and was due to start a business course at Brighton University next September. Her father had never had the chance to go to university himself and it was a matter of huge pride that Edward was going to be the first member of his family to get a degree. Kiri was longing to talk to her brother too. She wanted to hear all about working on a high-country farm in New Zealand.

'. . . to you too . . . glad to hear it . . . all well here . . .'

She almost snatched the phone from her father's hand. Her heart jumped at the sound of Eddie's excited voice.

'It's so cool here. The other guys are good fun, and we get to round up five thousand sheep with quad bikes and a helicopter!'

'No horses?'

'Horses too, but none as good as Foxy. Is he well?'

'He's fine.' Kiri's mouth trembled. She didn't want Eddie to know how close she'd come to harming his horse. 'I gave him extra carrots from you.'

'Thanks. I know you're doing a great job.' Guilt stabbed at Kiri as she handed the phone back to her father and she resolved to be a better person all round, starting right now.

She'd been dreading the present opening ceremony, but it went better than she expected. Steph put on a good act, pretending to like the perfume Kiri had chosen for her, and her father was all smiles when she gave him his framed photo of her and Eddie in the surf. Kiri had buried the faint hope that he would buy her a new pony, and there wasn't one. But he came up with something completely unexpected: a pocket-sized camera with a giant-sized zoom.

'I know how you love the marshes,' he said. 'Now you can record every inch of them.' She jumped up and kissed him before tackling Steph's present. She had a sinking feeling as she opened the elaborately wrapped box and delved though layers of crisp tissue paper. If it was a frilly dress, she'd die rather than wear it. There *were* frills, but on a white silk shirt instead of a dress and so she managed to keep a smile on her face when she changed into it for Christmas dinner.

Steph wasn't any more of a cook than her father so Kiri struggled to produce an overcooked turkey dinner. At least the roast potatoes and gravy turned out perfectly – just as her mother had taught her. While Steph and her father collapsed on to the sofa in front of Christmas TV, Kiri slipped out of the house to go to the stables. She was surprised to see snow falling. No one had forecast a white Boxing Day. She hurried across the field, leaving green footsteps in a thin blanket of white.

As soon as she opened the barn door, she knew something was terribly wrong. Foxy was standing motionless with his head down, sweat dripping from his neck. Shudders rippled along his body and his eyes were glazed with pain. Guilt gripped Kiri's heart with an iron fist – this was her fault. She knelt swiftly to remove his bandages and ran her hand down his tendons to see if one of them was damaged. A ruptured tendon would be agony, but his legs felt firm and healthy.

'Where are you hurting?' she begged. If only horses could tell you what was the matter. And then he did. He picked up one of his hind legs and kicked at his own belly. Colic. Kiri felt her own stomach cramp at the thought of it. What for humans might be no more than a severe stomach pain could be fatal in horses. If they rolled in agony from the pain, they could twist their intestines and die. Surgery could be attempted but often horses died a few days after the operation.

Eddie had often lectured her on the risk of colic. He'd hammered home the need for swift pain relief and drugs to stop the spasms inside the gut. He'd know what to do, but he was twelve thousand miles away. And although her father knew how to deal with emergencies on a building site – he'd once saved the life of a man bleeding to death – he was useless with animals. Kiri felt alone and helpless. It was Christmas night in the middle of the marsh in a snowstorm. How could she save Foxy?

The pain came in waves of mounting intensity. First a gripe in his belly. Then a cramp, which felt as if his guts were being turned inside out. Then a burning sensation like liquid fire, which made him sweat and shiver. It was unendurable. He kicked uselessly at his belly but nothing would stop the agony. Unless she could . . .

Chapter 3

Brrr . . . Brrr . . . The ringtone went on and on. Kiri was standing in the middle of the field – the only place she could get a signal near the barn. Her icy fingers were gripping her mobile hard enough to crush it, and the screen was blurring under thick snowflakes.

She'd turned the tack room upside down in a frantic search for Eddie's first aid box. It was on the high shelf where it was always kept – only she'd been too panicked to think straight. When she eventually found it, she upended the contents on to the tack room table and scrabbled through bandages, tape and disinfectant until she found a packet of what looked like equine medicine. But it was hopeless: she didn't know what it was for or how much to give, and Foxy could die of shock if she gave him the wrong drug or the wrong dose. She had to talk to a vet even if it was impossible for him to reach Walland Farm in the snow.

At last she got an answer, but it was only a recorded message. 'For our emergency service, please call . . .' The voice gabbled a string of numbers and Kiri cursed. Why hadn't she thought to bring a pen? She ran back to the stable where Foxy was moving restlessly and kicking at his belly. Time was running out. Grabbing a ballpoint and a torch, she ran back to the trampled patch of snow in the middle of the field.

This time she managed to write the emergency number on the palm of her hand but when she rang it, there was yet another recording: 'Leave your name and number with a brief description of the problem and a vet will call you back.' By now, Kiri was trembling with cold as well as panic, and she could hear her voice shaking as she left her message. She was desperate to get back to Foxy but she didn't dare. What if the vet returned her call while she was out of range? They'd probably think it was a prank and would never call again.

The snow eddied round her and mingled with the tears now pouring down her face. It seemed like hours before her phone rang, but she felt a surge of hope when she heard the voice of Mike Sweeting, the vet who'd looked after Mouse and Foxfire ever since they'd been at Walland Farm. She'd been afraid it would be an emergency vet who'd have no idea who she was, or how to find the farm.

'It's Foxfire. He's got colic,' she said in a voice shrill with fear. 'He's really bad and it'll be my fault if he dies. I know it's Christmas and I'm sorry, but there's no one else I can ask for help . . .' She couldn't go on because her chattering teeth and sobs threatened to overwhelm her.

'Slow down, Kiri,' said Mike. 'You've done the right thing to call me. Together we'll do everything we can for Foxfire. But first you need to describe his symptoms.'

Kiri was grateful to Mike for not patronizing her by promising that everything would be OK. She took a deep breath and told him about the sweating, the kicking and the glazed eyes. 'He's hurting badly inside, I know he is.' There was a brief pause and her stomach turned over for fear that Mike would say nothing could be done.

'We can deal with the pain but there's a problem. I'm already out on a call to an injured animal. So I can't get to you for another two hours, or even longer in this snowstorm.'

His words sent Kiri's brief surge of hope spiralling into despair. 'He might die before you get here.' Then she remembered the packet in the first aid box. 'I think we've got some painkiller. I know we're not supposed to have prescription medicines, but can I give it to him myself?'

There was a long pause before Mike answered. 'Tell me what's written on the label.'

'I can't!' Kiri explained about the barn's lack of mobile coverage in a voice choking with impatience. It was like a nightmare where she wanted to run but her feet wouldn't move.

Mike told her he'd wait for her to call him back. She ran to the barn, scooped up the packet and re-dialled his number as she stumbled back into the field.

'Well done,' he said. 'Read me the printing on the label.'

Kiri couldn't pronounce the word so she spelt it out: 'F I N A D Y N E.'

'That's good. It's a strong painkiller in a paste. You'll have to give it to him in the same way you give a wormer, or any other medicine. Have you got anyone to help you?'

'There's my father.'

'You've seen me and Eddie do this lots of times, so you should be fine. But remember your own safety comes first. If you think you're in danger because Foxfire might kick you, wait until I arrive. I'll come as fast as I can.'

He rang off and Kiri was left standing alone in the snow. She walked back to the barn, her heart thumping. She'd seen Eddie administer wormers: watched him put the paste into a big plastic syringe and slide it into the side of a horse's mouth. The trick was then to pump the medicine on to the back of the tongue so the animal had no choice but to swallow. That was the theory but she'd never actually done it herself – even to Mouse – let alone to a big horse thrashing around in pain.

She wondered whether to wake her father. But that would lose more precious time and he knew less than she did about horses. Inside the barn, Foxy was kicking at his belly all the time and his eyes were begging her for help. Kiri was paralysed by fear. Eddie had always been around before to sort out anything difficult or dangerous, but now there was only her.

'You've got to do it,' she told herself. 'This is your mess and you'll have to find the courage to get out of it.' She picked up the worming syringe and filled it with the painkiller but when she got back to the stable things had got worse. Foxy was starting to kick out to the side and she held her breath as she darted, past the flashing hooves, to his head.

'Trust me, Foxy. Please.' She managed to slip the halter over his ears and pushed the syringe into the side of his mouth with shaking hands. As soon as she pumped the medicine on to his tongue, he realized what she was doing and he didn't like it. He shook his head violently as he swallowed the paste, flinging her against the iron hayrack. She cried out in pain, but a cracked rib wouldn't matter if Foxy got better.

He swung his head round to bite his own flank and then the worst happened. His front legs buckled and he dropped to the floor and started rolling. The iron-shod hooves scythed to and fro as he twisted violently to try and escape the pain. He had to be stopped but every time she leant forward to grab the halter, he thrashed about and his hooves came within millimetres of scalping her.

'Foxy!' she cried out and for a second he kept still – just long enough for her to seize the halter and pull his head up. 'Get up! Please!' He looked into her eyes and hauled himself off the ground. She rubbed his forehead and tried to calm him with soothing words to give the painkiller time to take effect. It didn't matter what she said – it was her tone of voice that counted – so she just gabbled whatever came into her head.

'Mum always joked that Eddie and I were changelings because of our passion for horses. No one else in the family could tell a fetlock from a pastern but horses were all we ever thought of. Then you and Mouse came to live at Walland Farm and everything was perfect until . . .'

Kiri bit her lip. If she thought about the time when her mother got ill, her voice would crack and alarm Foxy, who seemed to be getting calmer. She started counting the seconds and then the minutes. Ten minutes since he last bit his flank. Fifteen minutes since he kicked. His eyes had stopped rolling and suddenly he looked like the friend she knew instead of an animal driven mad by pain. The relief made Kiri tremble all over and she sank to her knees in the straw.

Her eyelids drooped and the next thing she heard was the sound of Mike's four-wheel drive revving up as it swung through the gate and parked in the field. She ran outside and her heart lifted at the sight of Mike's encouraging smile.

'The painkiller calmed him down,' she said, 'but will the colic come back?'

Mike ran an expert hand down Foxfire's side and got out his stethoscope. 'It would help if I knew the cause,' he told her. 'Was there any sudden change in diet or exercise?'

Kiri froze. She couldn't bear to admit what she'd done. It would make him despise her for ever. She opened her mouth to say no, when a memory of her mother stopped her.

'Everyone tells lies sometimes,' her mum had said. 'Lies told to protect someone else aren't so bad, but there are two people you should never lie to – your best friend and your doctor.' A vet was a kind of doctor. Kiri suddenly knew she had to tell Mike the truth.

'It was my fault,' she said in a low voice. 'I took him out on the beach and we galloped for miles. He was in a terrible state when we got back.'

'What did you give him?'

'Only a small bit of hay and no water until much later.'

Mike went on examining his patient. 'There's little doubt in my mind that your galloping caused the colic, but you did the right thing when you got back.'

'You won't tell Eddie, will you? Or Dad?'

'No need. I think you've learned your lesson the hard way. And you were brave to administer the painkiller by yourself – it saved his life.'

Kiri felt dizzy with relief. Foxy had survived and Mike was still speaking to her in spite of what she'd done.

He gave Foxy an injection to prevent any further spasms and packed up his stethoscope. 'Foxy should be fine from now on.' Mike gave her a pat on the back as he left. 'Call me if you're at all worried, but I don't think it'll be necessary. He should be back to normal by the morning.'

Kiri put her arms round Foxy's neck. She'd always loved him, and now that she'd galloped him into danger and dragged him back from the edge of death, the bond between them felt unbreakable. She left him to rest and walked back to the house through fresh snow.

It had been the longest night of her life and it seemed strange that her father and Steph knew nothing of the drama. She'd have to tell her father about the vet's visit because there'd be a big bill to pay for coming out on Christmas night, but she wouldn't tell him about her wild beach gallop. He was very demanding of his children and, now that neither Eddie nor her mother were here to back her up, she sometimes felt intimidated by him.

She went into the kitchen to pour herself a glass of juice and caught sight of a folder marked *Walland Farm Renovations for Ms Stephanie Eland*. Too tired to investigate further, she climbed the stairs slowly to her bedroom. But as she drifted into sleep, she asked herself: what renovations and why?

Chapter 4

When Kiri woke, the blanket of snow, which had covered everything in the night, was already shrivelling under a light rain. She went straight to the stables to find Foxy eating his hay and whinnying for breakfast as if nothing had happened. It felt weird – as if she'd dreamed the whole thing – but the empty packet of painkiller and the twinge in her ribs were proof of the life-threatening drama. She gave Foxy the light feed prescribed by Mike and turned him out in the field with Mouse, who looked at her reproachfully. His special Christmas breakfast had given him ideas above his station.

When she went back to the house, she was surprised to find no one up and even more surprised to see her father's car missing from the place where he always parked, outside the front door. Surely he and Steph hadn't gone away on Boxing Day without telling her? Perhaps they'd just gone for a short drive to look at the marsh before the snow melted.

Sitting down in the kitchen with a fruit and yoghurt breakfast, she opened the folder marked *Walland Farm Renovations* and spread the contents over the kitchen table. There were sketches of interior designs and a floor plan, which, for a minute or two, she didn't even recognize. When the truth sank in, she was stunned. Steph was apparently planning to take over her much-loved, if ramshackle, home. There was a computer mock-up of a kitchen – all stainless steel and granite – the kind of kitchen that someone like Steph, who hated cooking, had just for show. Even worse, the floor plan showed that the original dining room, which her mother had used for her studio and hadn't been touched since she died, was to be turned into an office.

Kiri felt sick. She adored Walland Farm. The home, created by her mother, was a hotchpotch of stuff collected from antique shops, boot fairs and the beach. It was untidy and unfashionable, but it was absolutely theirs. And now Steph was out to destroy it. Just at that moment there were footsteps on the stairs and Steph herself walked into the kitchen.

'How dare you?' shouted Kiri, waving the sketches in the air. 'This is our house and you've got no right to walk in and take everything over.'

'I'm not taking anything over. Your father said the house needed work and so I asked some friends of mine to come up with some ideas.'

'I hate them!' A surge of anger lifted Kiri to her feet and she ripped the plans in half. 'You want to get rid of Mum's kitchen and demolish her studio.' Tears of fury started to flow and she threw the bits of paper in Steph's face as she rushed out of the room.

She went straight to her secret place – the high platform in the barn, used to store hay. The bales made a perfect refuge, hiding her from the world and wrapping her in the sweet and comforting smell of dried grass.

Her tears stopped, but the thought of Walland Farm changing was like a storm rolling towards her across the marsh. What was going to happen to her mother's paintings if the studio was destroyed? As a painter, Sylvia Dering had never been very good at letting go of her work. A few watercolours had been given to friends but she'd never got round to having a proper sale in a gallery, so there were dozens of canvasses stacked at the end of the studio. Kiri liked the oils best because they caught the golden light on the marshes. She'd often asked for a painting of Mouse or Foxy but her mother just shook her head.

'Portraits of animals and people aren't my thing,' she'd said. 'I only do landscapes or seascapes, I'm afraid.' But a year before she died, she'd given Kiri a painting of heavy surf, pounding ashore in lines of white spray, against a dark sky. 'This is the best I can do for you,' she'd said with a smile. 'Hang it in your bedroom and you'll be able to imagine white horses in the waves.'

Kiri was brought out of her memories by the sound of her father's car returning. She went back to the house expecting complaints by Steph about her behaviour, but the mess of torn plans had been cleared up and nothing more was said.

'Did you find Harding in?' Steph asked her father.

'No. He's gone to Liverpool for a week, so I'll have to drive up there tonight and arrange a meeting as soon as possible.' He was frowning and rubbing his eyebrows – something Kiri had noticed he did when anxious. 'You can stay here with Kiri, can't you?'

Kiri opened her mouth to protest and expected Steph to do the same but she didn't.

'Of course I'll stay. We'll be fine.'

Kiri followed her father to the upstairs room, which he used as an office, and watched him print off sheets of figures from his computer.

'Why are you going?' she asked. Her father always took time off between Christmas and the New Year, and he'd invited Steph to come for Christmas, so there had to be a serious reason for leaving.

'I've got a problem with the finance for one of my building projects. I'll be back in a few days.'

A few days! Kiri groaned inwardly at the thought of all that time in the company of Steph, but she knew better than to argue or whine. An hour later, she and

Steph waved him goodbye.

Kiri felt awkward as they went back into the house together. She knew she ought to say she was sorry for having thrown the papers in Steph's face, but she was still furious about the plans. To her surprise, Steph was the first to apologize.

'I'm sorry you found the plans before I had time to explain. And they were just ideas. The only thing that's really got to go is that hot water system.' As she spoke, the boiler gave a groan, which echoed through all the pipes in the house. They both laughed.

'Sorry I threw that stuff in your face,' said Kiri quickly, but inside she still felt bitter.

The next morning she wandered round the garden staring at the farmhouse with its mellowed bricks, its cat-slide roof and the porthole window beside the front door. It had been her mother's childhood home too, and Kiri didn't want anything to change: not even the peeling blue paint on the windows and doors.

The only way to avoid worrying about the house was to bury herself in her books on horse training. She'd already read her brother's manual on Portuguese dressage, which he'd used to teach Foxy tricks like the classical 'levade', where the horse rears when touched on the chest with a schooling whip. Kiri had taken the lesson even further, teaching Foxy to rear at the sound of her clicker, a small metal device for training dogs. But she'd never properly tried 'horse whispering' – using body language to communicate with horses. When Eddie had given her a book on the technique for her birthday, she'd attempted it with Mouse, but he refused to cooperate. 'You need horse *shouting*!' she'd said in exasperation, and left him to doze in the sun. Somehow she'd never got around to trying it with Foxy but now seemed a good time. It would strengthen the bond between them and make riding him easier.

She went to the barn, took off his rugs and brushed him. He was a beautiful horse. His coat was a deep, flaming chestnut, and his mane and tail were long and thick, an inheritance from his Lusitano sire. The influence of his thoroughbred dam could be seen in his lighter build, which gave him speed and the floating paces that Eddie hoped would one day make him an eventing champion. It was a demanding sport, which required a horse to be a star in all three phases: dressage, showjumping and cross-country.

She let him out into the field, so she could watch him interact with Mouse. If she was going to be a horse whisperer, she'd have to learn their language. Eyes soft and slightly drooping meant a relaxed attitude. Head down was submissive, but head up showed a challenge. She could tell a lot from their ears because hearing was such an important sense in horses – vital for detecting danger. Ears back and flat to the head showed fear or anger, but ears turned back without being flat were quite different: they meant the horse was paying attention to what was behind him – the rider if he was being ridden. Ears pricked were obvious: the horse was alert and excited.

After observing them for an hour, Kiri took Foxy into the small, circular pen where they sometimes kept Mouse, to stop him eating too much grass. She wanted to try the horse-whisperer technique for getting a horse to accept a human as leader of the herd. Foxy had no tack on – not even a halter – and Kiri was equipped only with a short length of coiled rope, which she kept in one hand close to her body.

She stood in the middle of the pen and faced Foxy directly, looking straight into his eyes with a challenging stare. A slight gesture with the rope asked him to move forward, and they started a kind of dance. As long as Foxy kept his head up and his eyes averted, she asked him to move on. But whenever he swung a lowered head towards her, she spoke words of praise and turned sideways in an encouraging attitude. At last he came right up to her and stood still while she stroked his neck. This was the crucial moment. Would he follow?

She walked away from him at an angle, and he stayed close behind. A tingle of excitement shot through her body. She went on walking and, even when she changed directions several times, he followed her like a shadow.

Her heart bounded with the knowledge that he'd accepted her as the leader of his herd. She'd become a horse whisperer!

She carried on practising in the pen with Foxy. It was fun and an excuse for keeping out of the house, so she was taken aback when Steph invited her on a shopping trip.

'I need some things, and Ashford has a good range of designer outlets. Do you want to come?'

'No!' Kiri realized her answer sounded rude. 'I mean, no thanks. I've got so much to do with Foxy.'

'That's OK. You're an outdoors sort of person as much as I'm an indoors one. But promise me you won't do anything crazy while I'm out. Like gallop on the beach.'

Kiri went scarlet. 'How did you know?'

'I didn't, until Mike Sweeting told me. He's an old friend of mine, and he's worried about you. With your father so busy, and Eddie in New Zealand, he thought you needed someone to look out for you.'

'I can look after myself.'

'I'm sure you can. But don't go mad with Foxfire on the beach again – or at least, not today!' With a wave of her hand, Steph got into her bright red sports car and drove off, leaving Kiri in a panic. She wished Mike Sweeting had kept his mouth shut instead of giving away her secret. What if Steph told her father, or Eddie, about what she'd done?

Chapter 5

While Steph was out, Kiri decided to try something new with Foxy. She'd read about a trainer whose bond with his horse was so strong that he could ride without a saddle or bridle. But to do this, he said, you had to learn to listen – really listen – to your horse.

She took Foxy into the smallest field and climbed on to the gate to get on. She felt him shift uneasily as she slid her leg across his back, so she sat still and listened. What was he telling her? That this was different, something he wasn't used to. She spoke soft words of encouragement until he relaxed. Then she touched his sides with her legs and he moved forward in a walk. After several circuits she tried a trot and was surprised to find him much easier to ride bareback than Mouse. Although she was a long way from the ground, he had comfortable paces, which made it possible to sit deep and still. A few moments later she was cantering bareback and even popped over a low jump.

Abandoning a bridle was much more of a challenge but when she took it off, Foxy shook his head as if glad to be rid of it. Taking a deep breath, she climbed on to his back and rode round the field using only her legs and shifts in body weight to guide him. The sense of horse and rider being at one was magical and she knew Foxy felt the same. There was a big mirror, which Eddie had rescued from a skip and put up in a corner of the field. As she rode towards it, she saw that Foxy had pricked ears and a freely swinging neck, while her own face had a grin as wide as the Cheshire Cat. She'd become a horse listener, as well as a whisperer.

She left Foxy to graze with Mouse and decided to go to Camber. She was bored with being stuck on her own, except for Steph, and she might see some of Eddie's friends on the beach. Camber was one of the longest stretches of sand in England and, although it seldom had huge surf like the beaches in Cornwall, it was ideal for kite surfers. Three of them were out in their wetsuits, despite the cold. She watched them gripping the lines that controlled their enormous kites and using the power of the wind to skitter across the waves on their surfboards. Riding a horse like Foxy across country would feel like that.

There was no one she recognized there, and loneliness overwhelmed her like a rogue wave. Most of the time she could cope with missing Eddie, but there were moments when his absence, and the loss of her mother, made her feel as if she was drowning. Two years ago, she would have been able to confide in her best friend, Kate, who was pony mad too. But Kate's family had moved to Yorkshire and a friendship on Facetime just wasn't the same.

After her mother died, Kiri's father had sent her to a boarding school near Ashford, because he was often away on business. He said she would make new friends there, but she hadn't. Too wrapped up in misery to make the effort, she'd ignored overtures of friendship and let herself drift into isolation. The new term would start in a few days' time and she wasn't looking forward to it. She'd miss the horses, and she felt sorry for them because Tom, the man her father paid to feed them when she was at school, didn't give them as much love and attention as they got from her.

By the time she arrived home, Steph's sports car was already parked outside the front door, and when she walked into the kitchen, she found the table laid.

'My turn to be chef this evening,' Steph called out from the sitting room. 'I bought something special because Jim's coming home tonight.' Kiri walked into the room and saw a froth of shopping bags and clothes strewn across the sofa and chairs. Her eyes locked on to a skater's skirt from Abercrombie & Fitch. Steph had a good figure, but surely she wasn't going to wear anything as short as that.

'Is that . . .' Kiri bit off the rest of the sentence, and blushed when she met Steph's amused glance.

'It's not for me, and I wouldn't buy anything like that for you. But there is something for you here.' She rummaged among the parcels and came up with a plain white box, which she handed to Kiri.

'For me?' Kiri couldn't keep the surprise out of her voice. It was a long time since she'd had an unexpected present.

'Open it and see!'

Kiri took the lid off and gasped as she pulled a gleaming new riding helmet out of the box.

'How did you know?'

'I saw how you had to cram your old hat on to the top of your head, and it didn't look like it was much protection.'

Kiri adjusted the straps and interior padding before putting it on and turning to look in the mirror. 'It's perfect.'

'I told the man in the shop I wanted something to suit a girl your age who was a risk-taker, and he said this was the one.'

'Thank you, but I can't . . .'

'Of course you can accept it. If your father wasn't so wrapped up in his business, he'd have got you what you needed. It just took a woman to notice.'

Kiri's head was all over the place: grateful that someone had noticed, worried that her thrifty father would disapprove and suddenly suspicious that Steph was trying to buy her affection.

They went into the kitchen where Steph opened the fridge with a flourish. 'We're eating sushi,' she announced.

'That's Japanese, isn't it?' asked Kiri, with a sinking feeling in her stomach. 'Raw fish?'

'Try it and see. It looks as if Jim will be late, so we won't wait for him.' Steph unpacked a takeaway, the like of which Kiri had never seen before. There were tiny balls of rice mixed with spices, exotic pieces of fish and toasted seaweed. After the first few mouthfuls, which Kiri gulped down fast to avoid being sick, she found she liked the taste after all. She dipped the morsels in soy sauce and enjoyed the strangeness of it.

'You've been to Japan, haven't you?' she said.

'I went there for my fashion company.'

'Dad said you'd sold your business.'

'I had to: to pay off debts that my husband ran up on my account. But if the divorce case goes the way I hope, I'll have enough money to start another business. That's why I've been buying all this stuff – to show my designers what's selling over here.'

Before Kiri could ask any more questions, the front

door banged and her father strode into the kitchen with a frown on his face. After kissing them both, he sat down and poured himself a large Scotch. 'No sense in beating about the bush. I went to see Harding, but he couldn't, or wouldn't, help. And without a loan from him, I'm in deep trouble. I won't be able to pay Eddie's university fees. He'll have to take out a student loan like his friends.' His voice grated as if he was angry, but Kiri knew it was only because he hated breaking promises. 'And you may not be able to keep going to that fancy boarding school of yours.'

'I don't mind – I don't like . . .'

Kiri's father shook his head. 'You can start the term and we'll see what happens. But don't count on staying.' The corners of his mouth turned down in an expression Kiri knew of old. Her father was a proud man who didn't like admitting defeat.

'I'll break the bad news to Edward straight away.' He glanced at his watch. 'It's already morning in New Zealand.'

It took a while to get through but as soon as Eddie picked up, her father went straight to the point, telling him to apply immediately for a student loan. Kiri was about to ask if she could talk to her brother when there was an explosion of rage from her father.

'Don't be an idiot! Of course you're going to university . . . absolutely not . . . I won't have it . . .

you're behaving like a fool.' He broke the connection and sat down heavily. 'Edward doesn't want to go to university now. He wants to stay in New Zealand and get an apprenticeship as a jockey. He says he'll start saving so he can pay me back the money I gave him for the airfare.' He plunged his head in his hands and groaned.

As Steph put her arm round her father's shoulders, Kiri slipped quietly out of the room and went upstairs with her head spinning. The prospect of her brother staying in New Zealand made her feel as if she was falling into another black hole. But if Eddie really decided to become a jockey on the other side of the world, he wouldn't need a horse at Walland Farm, would he? Foxy could become hers. Wanting Eddie to come home but longing to have Foxy for herself kept her emotions see-sawing late into the night.

It was still dark when Foxy lifted his head to sniff the breeze blowing in from the sea: a tang of salt, the sweetness of thyme and the reek of tar. He was looking forward to breakfast, and to seeing the girl. Memories of the boy were fading, and she was now the big presence in his life. He liked her gentle hands, her soothing voice and her soft hair that smelled of herbs.

Chapter 6

Kiri woke at dawn and crept out of the house to the barn, her heart beating fast. Now that Eddie wasn't coming home, she had to prove to herself that she was capable of being his rider. But would Foxy behave, or would there be another terrifying bolt? She tacked him up quickly, promising him, and herself, an extra large breakfast after their ride. As soon as she mounted, he started to paw the ground so she decided to give the beach a miss. Instead, she chose a bridleway, which went across the marsh. There was a surge of power as he moved into an extended trot, but this time she asserted herself as boss and a gentle but firm touch on the reins brought him back to a walk.

Confident now in her ability to stay in control, she started to look around and enjoy the ride. Walland Marsh had once been under the sea, and although it had been reclaimed hundreds of years ago, a shift in the light could turn the wide, flat spaces back into water. It was a place for giants, where electricity pylons marched across the land like an army, and wind turbines waved their arms angrily at mere humans.

Their route would take them past the wind farm in the middle of the marsh, and she wasn't sure how Foxy would react. Her breathing quickened and her grip on the reins tightened as she saw the huge blades turning slowly above her. She felt his muscles bunch and a sudden leap in the air almost threw her off. For a second she thought he was going to bolt. Then she realized he was just having fun, jumping the moving shadow of the blade.

The ride was going so well that Kiri decided to go to the beach after all. She wanted to test their new partnership to the limit. Foxy snorted with excitement when she turned him on to the path leading to the sea, and, after they crossed the road and the dunes, he started fidgeting and dancing sideways. But this time she was in charge. Instead of a flat-out gallop, she held him in a steady canter, along sand flattened by the ebbing tide.

'I can do it!' she said to herself. 'I can ride him anywhere.' But she'd spoken too soon. While Foxy was cantering happily through the shallows, she'd failed to spot danger further out. The kite surfer didn't seem dangerous at first – he looked competent – and she could see he was about to head back out to sea. But at the last minute, his kite dipped in the wind and swooped towards them like a bird of prey. Foxy reared, jinxed sideways and started to bolt.

Kiri felt a stab of panic – was this Christmas Day all over again? No! Now, if ever, was the moment to make use of all those hours she'd spent creating a bond between them. She had to listen to Foxy – think herself inside his head and understand him. If he saw the kite as a dinosaur about to sink its claws in his back, it was up to her to persuade him otherwise. She sat up in the saddle, tugged at the reins and spoke his name over and over again. At first he tried to yank her out of the saddle, but when she sat firm and kept her voice calm, he came back from gallop to canter, and then to a walk.

'Good boy,' said Kiri, stroking his neck and muttering more endearments. 'What a brave horse!' And he had been brave. Foxy had sensed her lack of fear and allowed the bond between them to bring him to his senses. They were a partnership!

When she got back to the farm, she longed to tell her father and Steph how well the ride had gone, but she didn't get the chance. As soon as she opened the kitchen door, she sensed an atmosphere.

'You're being unreasonable,' said Steph, pulling on her Burberry. 'I'll call you when I'm back in New York.' She gave Kiri a quick hug. 'Good luck with the riding!'

And she was gone, leaving Kiri's father looking even grimmer than before.

Kiri wondered what was going on. She felt a flare of protective love for her father and a surge of anger against Steph, who had no right to barge her way into his life and then disappear as soon as things got difficult. Kiri longed to ask if she'd gone back to the States for good, but didn't dare. Instead, she cooked her father's favourite breakfast of streaky bacon and scrambled eggs to cheer him up. Although he smiled and thanked her, his skin was taut, and his eyes seemed to be focussed elsewhere. Soon afterwards, he went for a walk, telling her he needed some fresh air.

While he was out, Kiri decided to call Eddie. If she could persuade him to change his mind about university that would really cheer her father up. And if Eddie came home, perhaps they could share Foxy. There wasn't enough money left on her mobile, so she took the house phone up to her bedroom and dialled New Zealand. It would be the middle of the night there, but she didn't care.

'Kiri! What's wrong?' Eddie's voice sounded sleepy and anxious.

'Sorry to wake you but I'm worried about Dad. He's got this trouble with the business, and now Steph's gone back to America.'

'For good?'

'I don't know. But I do know how much he wants you to come home and do that course at Brighton.'

There was a long silence before Eddie spoke. 'I was only going there because Dad wanted it. I'd much rather get a job and start paying back the money he gave me for the airfare.'

'Can you get a job in New Zealand?'

'One of the guys on the farm here has got an uncle who's a trainer. If he takes me on as an apprentice, I could be racing next year! It's the career I've always wanted.' Kiri could hear the excitement in his voice. 'Sorry to leave you on your own, but this is a great chance for me.'

'What about Foxy?' Kiri was trembling with hope.

'He can have a year off. You mustn't ride him yourself. He's too strong, and you promised. I'm holding you to that.' Now it was impossible for Kiri to tell him the truth, or ask him if she could have Foxy for herself. She ended the call feeling a complete failure. She hadn't been able to persuade Eddie to come home, and she'd lacked the courage to tell him the truth about her and Foxy.

Chapter 7

After three days back at school, Kiri was pining to be home again with the horses. So when her father arrived to say she would have to change schools, it was hard to stop the delight showing on her face.

'The headmaster said I could have some leeway,' said her father. 'You could stay for this term in the hope that my business would pick up. But I don't want to get into deeper debt.' Kiri understood how much it hurt him to say this. But she was relieved. However tough it might be to change schools, at least she would have the solace of living at Walland Farm and seeing Foxy and Mouse every day.

They put her luggage in the car and drove for a while in silence.

'I've arranged for you to start at the local school, Denge Academy, on Monday,' he said at last. Kiri could tell from his gruff tone of voice that he felt he'd let her down.

'Don't worry, Dad.' Kiri knew it would be hard. Starting mid-year in any school was difficult, and the other children would mock if they found out she'd come from an expensive boarding school. But she was determined to put a brave face on it.

'Marjorie, who's stayed with you before, will spend the night at the farmhouse whenever I have to be away.'

As soon as they had parked outside the farmhouse, they heard the landline ringing, and her father hurried indoors to answer it. Kiri jumped out of the car and went straight to the stables. Mouse whinnied to her from the field before putting his head down again to graze, but there was no sign of Foxy. She searched all the paddocks and trudged down to the shelter, which Eddie had built in the far corner of the big field, to give the horses shade in high summer. They seldom went inside in winter, but it was worth a check. Nothing.

A small worry started to flutter inside her chest. Of course she was being silly. Tom had probably left Foxy in his stall: either because he thought the horse needed extra hay, or because he just forgot to turn him out. Tom was getting on a bit, as he said himself, and sometimes got in a muddle.

Kiri ran to the barn and swung the door wide open. Foxy's stall was empty. The flutter in her lungs turned into a violent flapping of wings. She could hardly breathe as she rushed outside and ran along the boundary of their land to see if there was a break in the fencing where he could have escaped. If he had got out, where would he have gone? The beach? She gulped as she thought of the busy road he would have had to cross. The marsh was less dangerous, but it was a vast area to search.

Panting with anxiety, she completed the circuit of the fields without finding any gaps and a new, more frightening thought exploded inside her head. Had he been stolen? She ran to the tack room, unlocked the door with shaking hands and there was the evidence: Foxy's saddle and bridle were gone too. Only his halter remained, hanging from the brass hook as a cruel reminder of his absence. A terrible sound tore out of her lungs, like the cry of a mother whose child has disappeared. The thought of Foxy in the hands of thieves, perhaps already on his way to another country, made her heart judder. She ran to the house shouting incoherently.

'Help, Dad! Foxy's been stolen. We've got to call the police. Quick!' She pulled her mobile out of her pocket, but before she could dial 999 her father grabbed it out of her hand.

'He's not been stolen.'

'Where is he then?'

'Sold. I wanted to tell you before you ran to the

stable, but the phone rang . . . I didn't get a chance.'

'*Sold?*' The word stuck in her throat like a pill too big to swallow. 'You can't have sold him. You can't.'

'Edward isn't coming back any time soon. And we can't afford to keep an expensive animal like that.'

'But I *love* him! Where's he gone? I've got to go and see him.'

'Better if you don't.'

A cry of agony ripped out of her as she pushed her father away and ran for the sanctuary of the hay store. She crouched between the bales with tears washing down her face and her body shaking with sobs. When she'd cried herself dry she climbed down from the platform and went back to the house, hoping, against all likely hope, that her father would change his mind and cancel the sale.

'Can't you get him back?' Her voice cracked.

'I'm sorry. The deal is done.' He was speaking with the harsh tone he always used when breaking bad news. 'He was Edward's horse; I didn't realize you'd be so upset.'

'Of course I'm upset. I love him, and I hoped . . .' She stopped, unable to confess the wild hope she'd had of keeping Foxy for herself. 'It doesn't matter.'

'You matter,' said her father, reaching out to pull her into his arms.

'I don't matter to anyone.' She shrugged away from

him as her misery flared into anger. 'If you cared about me, you'd have known how much I love Foxy. And what about Mouse? He's too old to sell, so I suppose you're planning to put him down.' She wanted to hurt her father as much as she was hurting herself. 'You'd never dare do that if Mum was alive.'

Her father went white and reached out to her, but she pushed him away and ran back to the field to cry on the shoulder of her oldest friend.

'Foxy's gone, Mouse.' She put her arms round his neck and buried her swollen face in his mane. 'He's been sold and Dad won't tell me where he's gone.' She felt as if she was being sucked into yet another black hole. But something deep inside her said no. Not again. There was nothing she could do when her mother got sick, and nothing she could do when Eddie decided to stay in New Zealand. But she wasn't going to give up over Foxy. The thought of him lonely and unhappy in a strange place was unbearable. Somehow she'd find a way of getting him back. Impossible to imagine how – but the resolve was there, hard and unbreakable in the core of her being. As her tears started to dry, she saw her father walking towards her.

'You know I'd never do that to Mouse. He was a present to you from your mother, and I promised her – and you – that he'd have a home for life. And that's what he's got.' He patted Mouse on the nose and put an arm round Kiri as they walked back to the house.

'I didn't know how strongly you felt about Foxy. Truly. But even if I had, we couldn't have kept him as things are now. Feed, shoeing, vet's fees – keeping a big horse like that is an expensive business.'

'I know.' Although Kiri's anger with her father was still burning deep, there was a small voice inside her head, which said he hadn't meant to hurt her. But she couldn't forgive him, and she couldn't tell him the truth: that she was going to search for Foxy, buy him back and find a way of keeping him. Whatever that took. Her father and everyone else would rubbish her plan as a childish dream. But she knew better. It might take a miracle, but her love for Foxy was the stuff of miracles.

Foxy was bewildered. He'd been willing to walk into the horsebox and travel. He'd done that before. But the other times, he'd always come home again. For days he'd leaned over his new stable door, whinnying at anyone who came into the yard. But they never took him home. And they were never her. He gave up the whinnying and stood with his head drooping, abandoned.

Chapter 8

Kiri's new school was near Lydd, only a few miles from her home, so she could get there by bike every day. Her father had offered to drive her on the first day, but she told him she'd rather cycle. She didn't want to be seen arriving in her father's expensive four-wheel drive – it would make her seem too posh – and her classmates wouldn't know that it was about to be downgraded to a second-hand family car.

She was tall enough now to ride Eddie's bike, so she pulled it out of the shed and set off early. A low mist was curling across the marsh from the east, and a dawn glow from the horizon spiked the grass with tips of gold. Her mother had loved to paint at this time of day. Kiri liked to imagine that the mist was hiding the lost villages of the marsh – communities that had been destroyed by poverty or plague. She half saw shapes of vanished cottages in the haze, and heard the laughter of long dead children, running through the mist.

Denge Academy – named after the nearby Denge Marsh and predictably known as Dingy – brought her back into the modern world fast. Arriving after the start of term and missing some of the uniform was always going to be difficult, and Kiri took a deep breath as she was introduced to her new class. She kept a low profile through the first lessons and was grateful when a member of staff asked a girl called Tanya to keep an eye on her during the break. But Tanya made an excuse to disappear after a few words, leaving Kiri alone. She blushed under the scrutiny of older boys and felt herself shut out by groups of girls who'd known each other for years.

There was another loner in the playground, a girl of a similar age with black hair and a dark complexion, but when their eyes met, Kiri turned away. She didn't want to be identified with an outcast on day one. She struggled through the rest of the afternoon and hurried to get her bike as soon as she was free. The loner was standing beside it.

'Don't get on straight away,' she muttered out of the side of her mouth, in an accent Kiri didn't recognize. 'Someone's put a nail under your back tyre and it'll puncture as soon as you do.'

'Thanks,' said Kiri, feeling guilty about her earlier rejection of this girl. 'What's your name?'

'Roxana. Roxana Yonescu. But don't tell anyone it was me who warned you.' Roxana sidled away. Kiri was careful to lift her bike off the nail without looking as if she'd been given a warning.

She cycled home fast and went straight to see Mouse. He looked lonely in his field, and she ached with the realization that he missed Foxy as much as she did.

'How did it go?' asked her father when she went indoors.

'Good,' she lied. 'It'll be fine.'

They spent the rest of the evening in an uneasy silence, covered by the chatter of the television. Kiri was too choked up over Foxy to talk, and she guessed her father was obsessed by his business worries and the quarrel – if there had been a quarrel – with Steph. Waking up late the next morning, she only had time to give Mouse a quick check over before she had to start pedalling fast for Dingy. Roxana was waiting for her near the school gate.

'It's PE this afternoon, and you've got to have a navy tracksuit – I can lend you one if you like.'

'Thanks.' Kiri wanted to be friendly. 'Where are you from?' she asked, and was taken aback when Roxana went the colour of beetroot, turned on her heel and walked away.

'She's a Gyppo,' said Tanya, who'd overheard the

exchange. 'From Romania, like most of the illegals round here. Only they've made them legal now. Her mum's a housekeeper – that's posh speak for a cleaner – and her father's done a runner. You don't want to know her.'

Although the school bell saved Kiri from having to answer, she had already decided that Tanya was the one she didn't want to know. When she found the maths classroom, she made a point of going to sit next to Roxana even though she wouldn't have chosen the front row herself.

'I didn't mean to pry,' she whispered, but the teacher came in and there was no chance to say any more. In the break, she followed Roxana to the far side of the playground.

'The other kids will tell you I am an illegal, but I never was,' the girl said fiercely. 'And I'm not a Gyppo, or whatever names you English call us.'

'I'm not calling you anything,' said Kiri quickly. 'I don't know anything about you.'

'We're from Romania. My great-grandma's a real Roma – what some people call a gypsy – but my mother wanted to settle down. She wanted a flat to live in and a school for me, so we came to England eight years ago. She got a permit to work here and she pays taxes like everyone else. But since I moved to this school, the other students treat me like dirt.'

'Don't take any notice of Tanya and her friends. They're just prejudiced.'

'I hate them.'

Over the next few days, Kiri got to know Roxana better. She saw how the Romanian girl was shunned by most of the other students – unless they were making rude comments about her background and family. Roxana ignored them and kept her head held high and a fierce expression on her face, but Kiri could see how much it must hurt and admired the girl for her courage.

The two girls started to spend break times together. They were both reserved and reluctant to talk about themselves, until Kiri got emotional over a text from Eddie.

'What the matter?' asked Roxana.

'It's my brother, Eddie. He's fine, but he's in New Zealand. I miss him.'

'That's hard, but at least you've got a brother. There's just Mum and me at home – my father disappeared when I was young. Mum's the best in the world, but I'd love to have a brother or sister.'

'I'm on my own a lot now.' Kiri explained how her father had to spend weekdays in Liverpool, leaving her in the dreary company of Marjorie.

'Come back to our place for tea today,' said Roxana impulsively. 'Mum won't mind and she can take you home afterwards.'

'I'd like that, if you're sure it'll be OK.'

Roxana called her mother, and Kiri phoned Marjorie to tell her she wouldn't be home until later.

The two girls got the bus to Camber. Kiri was surprised when Roxana led the way to a holiday park. She got even more of a shock when Roxana unlocked the door of a decrepit wooden chalet. Inside, it was beautifully clean with bright rugs covering the shabby vinyl floor – but it was tiny. There was a living area with a sink and a cooker in the corner, a bedroom with a double bed, a shower room and another bedroom, which was so small that there was barely room for a single bed.

'Is this your room?' asked Kiri, looking at the posters of Romania on the wall.

'Mum makes me have the bigger room because it's got a desk for my homework. I wish we could afford a proper flat but we get this place cheap because Mum helps clean the holiday cottages.'

'It must be fun here in the summer.'

'Not really. We're not allowed to use the pool, and it's noisy. Kids yelling all day and their parents yelling back at them.'

At that moment, the door opened and a woman with Roxana's heart-shaped face and dark eyes came in.

'Kiri,' she said with a warm smile. 'Roxana's always talking about you.'

Marina insisted on Kiri calling her by her first name and invited her to share their meal of *clatite* – Romanian pancakes with a cheese filling. Kiri and Roxana tucked in and started chattering as if they'd known each other for years. After they'd eaten, Marina insisted on driving Kiri back to Walland Farm and made sure that Marjorie was waiting for her in the house.

'I start work late tomorrow,' said Marina, 'so I'll pick you up and drive you both to school. It'll be no trouble.'

Two weeks later, Kiri cycled home from school to find the house empty and no sign of Marjorie. She ate some pizza and settled down on the sofa with a book. Just after seven o'clock, Marjorie called to say she had a terrible stomach upset and couldn't come. She'd tried to call Kiri's father but couldn't get through. Kiri thought about phoning her father herself, but he'd only make a fuss, and the idea of spending a night by herself in Walland Farm was exciting, as well as scary. She went round checking the locks on all the doors and windows on the ground floor and then locked the upstairs windows as well. But when she got into bed with the duvet tucked up to her chin, she couldn't sleep for ghosts moaning in the attic, burglars tiptoeing up the stairs and smugglers clinking bottles under her window.

She decided the only way to defeat the noises was

to identify them. She closed her eyes the better to listen. The ghost was the cry of an owl gliding past her window. The burglars were just the creaks of an old house settling down for the night. The smugglers went on smuggling for a while, but at last she recognized the sound of a milk bottle, rolled to and fro by the wind on the paving stones below. Reassured, she allowed her imagination the luxury of inventing a dog curled up beside her on the bed, and fell asleep to the sound of its gentle breathing.

The next morning she woke up pleased to have got through the night and determined to get rid of Marjorie, who she'd never liked. As soon as she got to school, she explained the problem to Roxana.

'I know I can't go on being at home alone, so I wondered if you and your mother could come and stay?'

'When?'

'Tonight – if possible, and the next two nights.'

'Tonight?' Roxana sounded surprised.

'Only if you want to, of course,' Kiri added quickly.

'I'd love to.' Roxana's face was transformed by one of her brilliant smiles. 'But I don't know what Mum will say. I'll call her straight away.'

'Tell her Dad will pay for every night she stays,' said Kiri, blushing. She didn't like talking about money, but she knew the Yonescus were hard up.

Roxana couldn't get through until lunch break, when she came back to say she'd get the bus back to Camber as usual, and her mum would drive her over to Walland Farm when she finished work. She warned Kiri that her mother would insist on speaking to Kiri's dad before agreeing to stay.

Soon after Kiri got home, she heard the sound of a car pulling up at the front of the house. She opened the front door and saw Roxana and Marina getting out of a battered old Ford.

'I came as soon as I could when I heard you were on your own,' said Marina with a reassuring smile, 'but we must get your father's agreement for me to stay.'

Kiri dialled her father's mobile, hoping he'd be too busy to make difficulties.

'Hi, Dad. Marjorie didn't show up last night, but I was OK on my own. Now I've got my school friend, Roxana, with me, and her mother. She wants to talk to you.' She handed over the phone before he could protest, and listened as Marina gave explanations, contact details and a reference.

'I believe you know Dr Swanson?' she said. 'I have worked for her for two years – so please speak to her, and if you are happy with what she says about me, I will stay.' She gave the handset back to Kiri.

'It was very wrong of Marjorie to leave you alone all night,' said her father. 'I'll drive down tonight if you want, but if Dr Swanson gives a good reference and you're happy with Marina and her daughter, I'll stay in Liverpool until Friday.'

'Cool.' Kiri grinned at Roxana. 'I'm sure the doctor will say it's all right. While we're waiting for Dad to call back, you must come and meet Mouse.' She led the way to the field, where the pony honoured them by lifting his head from the grass to say hello.

'You're so lucky,' said Roxana, stroking his soft nose. 'I love horses but I've never even sat on one.'

Kiri took her to the hideaway among the hay bales, but when she looked down on the empty stall, she couldn't stop herself bursting into tears. Eventually the whole story of Foxy came out.

Roxana took Kiri's hands in hers. 'I'll help you get him back. Somehow. And we can ask my great-grandma. She's a real Roma, so she can look into the future and know what's going to happen.' She paused. 'Although she doesn't always tell people what she sees.'

The girls went back to the farmhouse and ate sausages and chips cooked by Marina, who said Kiri's father had called back to say he was happy with the arrangement. Marina was to go in the guest bedroom, and Roxana could have a mattress on the floor beside Kiri's bed.

When Kiri showed Roxana the room they were to share, her eyes widened.

'This house is like a fairy tale,' she said, looking at Kiri's pictures and books and the shelves with her collection of shells.

'This is my favourite painting,' said Kiri. 'My mum painted it for me before she died, so I could imagine white horses inside the waves.'

They talked late into the night and Kiri was amazed to think how fast her life had changed. A few weeks ago, she'd been lonely enough to cry, and now she had a new best friend.

'But I won't forget you, Foxy,' she promised silently. 'You're the most important thing in my life and Roxana and her great-grandma are going to help me get you back.'

Chapter 9

Kiri woke early as she had every morning since she discovered Foxy had been sold. She'd kept on asking her father for the name of Foxy's new owner, but he always gave the same answer: it was better if she didn't know. Last Sunday, just before he left for Liverpool, she'd asked yet again, even though she knew it would make him angry.

'I'm not telling you and that's an end of it,' he growled, frowning. He'd hugged her before he drove away, but Kiri knew she wouldn't dare ask again.

Now, lying awake and thinking of Foxy neglected and unhappy in a strange yard, she felt herself gripped by a new resolve. She was going to defy her father and find out where Foxy was, even if that meant going behind his back. She swung her legs out of bed, pulled on an old sweater and pushed her feet into her Crocs.

'Where are you going?' asked Roxana in a sleepy voice.

'My dad's office. I've got to find out who bought Foxy.'

'I'll come with you.'

The two girls crept out of the bedroom, so as not to wake Marina, and tiptoed along the passage to the office. Kiri's heart beat faster as she switched on the computer. She felt like a criminal, but it was her father's fault. If only he'd told her what she so desperately needed to know, she wouldn't have to hack into his emails. When the request for a password came up, she guessed her father would choose something obvious like the names of his family. Sure enough, after messing about with different combinations of Sylvia, Edward and Kiri, she got lucky with 'sylvedki', and the screen cleared.

'Are you sure about this?' asked Roxana.

'Absolutely. I'd never forgive myself if I abandoned Foxy.'

The mailbox opened and a list of emails flashed on to the screen. Her father must have decided to sell Foxy as soon as he knew that his business was in difficulties and Eddie wasn't coming home. She didn't think he'd have advertised in the horse magazines, and there hadn't been time for buyers to come round and try Foxy out. That meant the sale must have been to someone he already knew.

'Try that one,' said Roxana, pointing at an email which had 'Sale' in the subject line, but it was just a query about a building site. There was nothing for it but to open every email received in the last few weeks. It was slow work, but at last they found something that made Kiri's heart jump: an email from Grant Harding, the man her father had hoped would save his business. Although most of it was about property, there were a couple of sentences at the end, which made Kiri's spine tingle. 'I can't help your company, but I can do a deal on the other matter you spoke of. He sounds just right for my son, William.' Although there was no mention of Foxy or even the word 'horse', Kiri's instinct told her she was on the right track. She went into her father's file of contacts and found an address and postcode for the Hardings.

'I know where that is,' said Roxana. 'It's a road with lots of big detached houses just outside Rye – Mum does the cleaning in one of them.'

'Do they have stables?' asked Kiri.

'Google them and see.'

Kiri was already zooming in on the satellite view of the houses, and although they had big gardens, there were no fields or stables.

'The Hardings could be keeping Foxy in a livery yard, a riding stable that looks after horses for owners who can't do it themselves. It would probably be somewhere close.' She wanted to rush out and start looking straight away, but Marina would be up soon and they had to get ready for school. There was a bike rack on the back of Marina's car, so she was able to take both girls, and Kiri's bike, to the Academy. Because she was working late that afternoon, Kiri and Roxana would share Eddie's bike on the way home.

Kiri's impatience was getting the better of her by the lunch break. 'Let's bunk off school now,' she said, as they shared sandwiches and apples. But her friend's eyes rolled in shock at the suggestion.

'You've no idea what sacrifices Mum makes for my education. I can't let her down like that.'

Kiri got another surprise after school when she suggested Roxana should ride the bike while she jogged alongside.

'I don't know how,' Roxana explained. 'We've never been able to afford a bike. And it's a boy's bike! I'd have to hitch my skirt right up.'

'We'll do it like this then.' Kiri got Roxana balanced sideways across the luggage rack with her skirt neatly arranged over her legs and swung her own tracksuited leg across the bar. Roxana gave a shriek of fright as they wobbled off to a slow start, but she was laughing with excitement as they gained speed across the marsh. Kiri kept looking for a chestnut horse in the distance, even though she knew that seeing Foxy by chance was virtually impossible. It was hard work pedalling for two and she began to realize they'd never be able to visit all the local riding stables this way.

'Let's take a breather,' she said, braking gently so Roxana could jump off without tripping. They laid the bike on the grass and shared an apple, sitting on a hump-backed bridge over one of the wide ditches that drained the marsh.

'What's that?' asked Roxana, pointing at something shaking the reeds on the far side of the ditch.

Kiri stared, then jumped up to get a better view. 'Looks like something's stuck.' The ditch was deep, as well as wide, with a thick band of reeds on both sides. Kiri moved back up the track until she could see what it was. 'It's a dog! Trapped in the reeds.' She waited a few moments, hoping its feeble struggles would succeed in getting it free.'

'It can't get out,' said Roxana. 'It's going to drown.'

Kiri took off her shoes and tracksuit trousers and slithered down the side of the ditch. The ice cold water made her gasp; she knew the dog couldn't last long in this temperature. The ditch was even deeper than she expected, and she was up to her waist in the water when she reached the animal, which was looking at her with desperate eyes. She put her arms round its body and heaved. There was a slurping noise and the dog came out of the mud – stinking, glutinous mud – that now covered them both. Still clutching the animal, she dragged it to the bank, where Roxana was waiting to pull them out.

The cold had seeped into Kiri's body. She was shivering violently but so was the dog. It shook itself, sending water spraying in all directions. Kiri used her tracksuit trousers to towel its muddy coat as best she could. They all needed to get home fast. She pulled on the wet trousers and lifted the dog into the big carrier on the front of the bike, hoping it would have the sense to stay there.

'I can't manage you as well as the dog,' she told Roxana. 'I'll come back as fast as I can.' Roxana nodded, but her tight lips told Kiri she was nervous about being out on the marsh on her own. 'I won't be long, I promise.'

'Stay still!' she told the dog and started pedalling furiously. The road was flat and she quickly got up to a good speed. By the time she turned into Walland Farm, the exercise had warmed her up, although the dog was still shivering. At least its weakened state had stopped it jumping out of the basket. She carried it into the barn, made another effort to dry it with a towel and laid it in the straw of Foxy's stall.

'Back soon, dog,' she said, giving it a pat on the head. A quick change into a sweatshirt and some old jodhpurs took only a moment, and she was back on the road. She met Roxana walking fast towards her. Her friend's big smile told her how relieved she was not to be alone any longer. They cycled back to the barn, and found the dog, burrowed deep into the straw. Kiri got a bucket of warm water and gently washed off the mud, revealing a male Border collie with a red and white coat.

'Look how thin he is!' said Roxana.

'He's been beaten,' said Kiri, letting her fingers softly probe a welt on his back. She fetched two leftover sausages from the fridge, which were swallowed in a single gulp. He licked her hand and looked up at her with liquid brown eyes.

Roxana stayed in the barn while Kiri went back to the kitchen for more food. She knew the collie needed proper dog food, and plenty of it, but a tin of ham, which she'd found in a cupboard, would have to do for now.

They smuggled him into the house and up to their bedroom while Marina was cooking supper. His existence would have to be declared when Kiri's father came home on Friday but until then, he was their secret. He lay on Kiri's bed, staring at her with total trust, and a gently wagging tail.

'You saved his life,' said Roxana, 'and now he's asking you to give him a new one. You can start by giving him a new name.'

'I'll call him Ben.'

'Ben's a good name, but will your father let you keep him?'

Kiri's feelings for her father were all jumbled up. Long ago, when they'd been a complete family, she'd loved him in an uncomplicated way. Now that love was all mixed up with anger over Foxy, guilt about looking at his emails and anxiety about whether she could keep Ben. She sighed and ruffled the dog's coat.

'I'll know on Friday.'

Chapter 10

Kiri was seething with frustration. There were two more days of school to get through before the weekend gave her the chance to start looking for Foxy. She was convinced he had to be stabled somewhere nearby. She thought again about bunking off school in the afternoon, but Roxana would be shocked and if her father found out, she'd be in trouble. Enough trouble to set him against any plan of hers to keep Ben. So she stayed at school but found it impossible to concentrate. On Friday, she dragged Roxana to the back row where she passed notes and whispered until the exasperated teacher kept them in during the lunch break for talking in class.

'Sorry, that was my fault,' said Kiri. 'I get so bored in French and I always come bottom anyway.'

'Only because you don't try.' Kiri realized Roxana was upset because of the detention – her mother might get to hear of it. But she'd got used to total loyalty from her new friend and the criticism rankled.

'It's easy for you,' said Kiri. 'You speak lots of languages.'

'Nothing's easy for me! I have to learn everything – even maths – in a foreign language, and write essays using words I only half understand. And I don't have a huge house, with someone to cook meals for me. I have to help Mum clean some nights, and do the cooking if she's not in till late.' Roxana walked away, her face dark with anger.

Kiri was too surprised to stop her going. The jibe about the house made her feel uncomfortable but she resented the remark about cooking. She often had to make supper for her father and herself.

They avoided sitting together in the afternoon classes, and Marina picked Roxana up promptly at the end of school. Kiri cycled home feeling hard done by but, when she got to the barn and gave Ben a cuddle, she found she was missing her friend. The adventure of rescuing the dog with Roxana had been fun. In fact, everything had been more fun together.

As soon as she heard her father's car on the drive, she gave Ben a bowl of food and went to welcome him home. In the old days, she'd have thrown her arms rounds his neck but there was an awkwardness between them now.

'Hi, Dad.'

'Hello, darling. How was your week?'

'Good.' They talked of unimportant matters, like his drive down from Liverpool, and her school uniform, circling warily round the two things that neither dared mention: Foxy and the state of his business.

'I've bought pizza and ice cream. I'll do a proper shop tomorrow.'

'Can you buy some . . .' Kiri was about to say dog food. But she had to tell him about the dog first.

'Something happened on the way back from school.' The tone of her voice must have warned him that what she had to say mattered. He looked up, his eyes fixed on her face.

'Something good or something bad?'

'Both.' She was finding it hard to tell him about Ben, but in the end it all came out in a rush. 'Me and Roxana found a dog trapped in one of the ditches. It was stuck and drowning, so I got it out and brought it home.'

'And you want to keep it?'

Kiri nodded, unable to speak in case she started crying.

'We'll see. A dog's not just for Christmas, you know.' There was a smile on his face. Kiri knew he was thinking of the sticker her mother used to have in the rear window of her car.

They walked over to the barn and Ben jumped up and down with excitement. Although he was bone thin, he was a handsome dog. His ears were pricked and, after hours of detangling, his coat was silky.

'How could anyone resist those eyes,' thought Kiri. 'And that wagging tail.'

'He seems friendly,' said her father, 'and he's a good-looking dog, but we've got to find out if his owner is looking for him.'

'He was beaten and starving!'

'Not necessarily by his owner. He could have run away and been beaten by someone else.' He sighed. 'We've got to take him to the dog warden and get him checked for a microchip. But I agree with you – I don't think he's got one and I don't think he'll be claimed.'

Kiri's heart, which had done a somersault at the mention of a dog warden, went back to its normal rhythm.

'You'll have to wait several days before the warden will let you have him.'

'Does that mean I can keep him?'

'On condition you take full responsibility. You'll have to feed and exercise him every day. That means getting up very early before school to look after Ben, as well as Mouse.'

Kiri's heart leapt. 'I'll get a weekend job to pay for his food.'

Her father hesitated. 'That's a responsible attitude, but I don't want your schoolwork to suffer.'

'It won't,' lied Kiri. 'I'll do extra homework as well.'

Her father took her in his arms and gave her a big hug. 'I know how upset you were about Foxy, and you deserve to be happy. But don't run ahead of yourself. It'll be a while before we know whether you can keep the dog. I don't want you going through another heartbreak.'

Kiri was shaking with emotion: the excitement of keeping Ben, the fear that she might not be able to and guilt because she was planning to go behind her father's back to look for Foxy. For a moment she considered telling him about her plan, but of course she couldn't. He'd stop her. He was obviously hoping that looking after Ben would take her mind off Foxy, but that, she promised herself, was never going to happen.

The following morning, Kiri brushed Ben until he shone and threw one last ball for him before putting him in the back of the car.

'It's only for a few days,' she told him, hoping it was true, 'and then you'll be home for good.' They drove to the dog pound and handed him over to the warden. His large, trusting eyes looked back at Kiri as he was taken away to the kennels, and she had a sudden longing to snatch him back. It would be agony if a previous owner claimed him. After a quick shop at the nearest supermarket, they got into the car to drive home.

'When's Steph coming back?' Kiri saw her father's hands tighten on the steering wheel before he replied.

'I don't know. She's very busy in America with her divorce case.' He spoke in a tone of voice that meant the subject of Steph was closed.

Kiri didn't dare ask if his business problems were getting better or worse. What if they got so bad that he had to sell Walland Farm? Even if she had the courage to ask, he probably wouldn't tell her.

When they got home, her father went straight to his office, and Kiri got on her bike to ride to the stable yard nearest to the Hardings' house. It was up a steep hill; by the time she got there, she was panting with exertion and shaking with excitement at the thought of seeing Foxy. She pushed open the gate and ran into the yard, convinced she'd hear his welcoming whinny. Instead she almost crashed into a middle-aged woman, who pushed her aside angrily.

'Where do you think you're going?' she asked sharply.

'I've come to see William Harding's horse, Foxfire.'

'I don't know what you're talking about. There's no one of that name among my clients. Now please leave.' She gestured to one of her stable girls. 'Harriet, show this girl out.'

Kiri's face was flaming. What a horrible woman! And, to make matters worse, she could feel tears of desperation running down her cheeks.

'Do you know William?' asked Harriet.

'No. But he's bought my brother's horse. I just wanted to see if Foxy's all right.'

'It's hard saying goodbye to a horse.' Harriet gave a sympathetic smile. 'William used to keep a horse here a long time ago but he left. He's a good rider – unless his father's watching.'

'Do you know where he keeps his horse now?'

The girl shook her head. 'Somewhere near Ashford, I think. But I don't know where.'

Kiri freewheeled down the hill feeling crushed. She'd been so certain of finding Foxy near the Hardings', and if he was miles away in Ashford, it was going to be much harder to track him down.

Chapter 11

Bright sunshine the following morning sent optimism flowing back into Kiri's veins. She decided to call the local stables where she'd already done odd jobs, to see if they could give her regular weekend work. It would bring in money to pay for Ben's keep, and the owner, Aggie Vines, might be able to tell her the names of stables near Ashford. Torebridge was a small yard without the grand facilities that would attract serious competitors, but it was a happy place and Kiri had always enjoyed working there. She got through to Aggie at once.

'Have you got any work going?'

'You've called at the right moment,' said Aggie. 'My stable girl has just walked out and my new manager needs all the help she can get.'

Her father gave her a hug when she told him where she was going. 'I hope you get the job,' he said, 'but don't forget what I said about homework.'

Kiri cycled the five miles to Torebridge at breakneck pace. Twenty wooden loose boxes were laid out in a square, next to an ugly bungalow that was Aggie's home. There was a caravan for the stable girl and a sand arena for schooling and lessons. The best thing about Torebridge was its land – enough grazing for the horses to be turned out every day, and space for a set of showjumps and some cross-country obstacles. As Kiri pushed her bike through the gate, she was surprised to see a large, but ancient, horsebox parked on the far side of the bungalow. Aggie, a wiry woman with grey hair and a weather-beaten face, nodded towards it.

'That belongs to Jen, my new stable manager. She's got all kinds of plans for this yard, and you can see she's already smartening the place up.'

Aggie was right. One row of stables had already been given a new coat of wood stain and the doors had new bolts and hinges. 'I can't offer you any paid riding – it'll mostly be mucking out.'

Kiri had been expecting that. Most of the clients at Torebridge were on a tight budget and did their own exercising. That would leave her with raking the sand arena, mucking out stables and the job known as 'poo-picking': going round the fields with a shovel and a wheelbarrow to clear up horse droppings. Kiri didn't mind. She'd rather clean up after horses than humans.

She'd once had a job cleaning holiday cottages and been disgusted by the mess holidaymakers left behind.

'How much do you pay?' asked Kiri, thinking of the price of dog food.

'The minimum wage for your age group is all I can manage, but I'll try to let you take Greyling out for a ride sometimes, as an extra.' Greyling was Aggie's old hunter. Like his owner, he was too stiff to go far or fast these days, but any riding was better than none.

Kiri started on the mucking out. The first box was occupied by a horse she'd never seen before: a black thoroughbred gelding, which Aggie had told her belonged to the new manager. The horse looked a lot classier than Torebridge's usual lodgers, but he was standing at the back of the box with his ears back and his teeth bared. Kiri tipped her head on one side and wondered what he was trying to say to her. 'Get out of my space!' for sure. But why? Perhaps he'd been badly treated in the past. She went into the loose box slowly and looked the horse steadily in the eye. When he eventually dropped his gaze, she turned her head away, inviting him to come closer. She was using the same technique that had persuaded Foxy to follow her in the field and, although the box was too small for proper horse whispering, she seemed to have established a relationship. She waited until she felt the animal's breath on her neck. Hoping his teeth were no longer bared, she turned slowly round and patted him on the shoulder. The ears were now forward and she spent several minutes caressing his neck and speaking softly to him.

'Well done. Tanker doesn't usually allow strangers in his box.' A girl of about twenty-five with short, honey-coloured hair and grey eyes was leaning on the stable door. 'I'm Jen, the new manager here.' Jen came inside the box, and Kiri felt the tension easing from Tanker's muscles as he took some sliced carrot from the girl's hand.

'Why's he called Tanker?'

'Because he likes to tank off with his riders and throw them in a hedge! I got to buy him cheap because I was the only one who could stay on. He's fine with me now – most of the time – but I don't let anyone else ride him.' Jen showed Kiri which boxes needed mucking out and asked her to rake the sand in the schooling arena. 'Come to the living area of my horsebox when you've finished, and I'll make you a hot drink.'

Three hours later, Kiri was drinking hot chocolate and hearing about Jen's plans.

'This yard could do really well because of its fantastic location. You can get horses fit on the beach, or the Downs, and it's got enough space for a cross-country course. I can offer coaching in dressage, as well as jumping, and Aggie says that will attract new clients who are interested in competing. Then, as more money comes in, we can start making improvements.'

'I know of someone who might be looking for a competition yard.' Kiri felt her breath taken away by her own daring. 'He's called William Harding; he's just bought my brother's horse.'

'I know William,' said Jen. 'He tried to chat me up at an event last year.' She was smiling at the memory. 'He's too young for me, but he's a good rider, especially on the flat. He keeps his horse at a yard near Ashford, but he told me it was a long way to drive every day.'

'So he might be glad to come here.' The thought of luring William to Torebridge and being able to see Foxy whenever she wanted was making Kiri breathless.

'He's serious about eventing and his father's got lots of money, so he wouldn't normally consider a small yard like this. But he *did* once say he'd like me to give him some coaching.' Jen's eyes were bright with amusement. 'Although I'm not sure what kind of coaching he had in mind.'

'Do please ask him to bring Foxy here.'

'It would be a long shot. But if he came here and won an important event as my pupil, other riders might be impressed enough to bring their horses here too.' Jen pulled herself back from her daydream of a dazzling future for Torebridge. 'What's his horse like?'

'Foxy's the most beautiful horse in the world: a fiery

chestnut with a long "Luso" mane. He's half Lusitano and half thoroughbred. And he's got talent – he can do anything.' Tears welled as Kiri thought of the hours she'd spent brushing that silky mane.

'Why was he sold?'

'My father's business is in trouble, and when my brother decided to become a jockey in New Zealand . . .' Kiri's voice cracked. 'Dad said we couldn't afford to keep a horse like that.'

Jen leant forward and gave Kiri a tissue to dry her eyes. 'Having him here might be hard for you. He's William's horse now, and you'd have to accept that.'

'I could cope with that. As long as I can see him every weekend and help look after him.'

'Mm. William has a reputation for being difficult. So, if he does bring Foxy here – which isn't very likely to be honest – I hope you won't regret it.'

Kiri was humming with excitement as she cycled home. She'd discovered where Foxy was being kept, and she had a gut feeling that her plan to bring him back to the marshes would work. Jen's comment about William being difficult cast a shadow over her good mood, but what if he was? It didn't matter if he was rude or bad tempered. All she cared about was having her arms round Foxy's neck again.

Foxfire thrust the whole of his weight against the stable

door without making it give an inch. Angry that his strength wasn't enough, he closed his jaws over the rim of the door to shake it loose, but his teeth scraped on metal and his tongue recoiled from the bitter ointment smeared along the top. Poison! He flung himself to the back of the box and stood there with nostrils flaring and muscles quivering. There was a net full of sweet hay hanging from the wall, but he wouldn't eat. Not until he found a way out of his prison. The people here brought feed and water at regular intervals and exercised him every day in an indoor school but what use were hours of boring circles inside a building? He wanted the salt smell of the marshes and the flash of waves under his hooves. More than anything, he wanted her. The one who was firm but gentle. The one who understood.

Chapter 12

Kiri went back to school bursting with news about Ben, her new job and her scheme to bring Foxy to Torebridge. She was so keen to tell Roxana everything that she forgot about their quarrel. But as soon as she saw her friend turn away, she remembered.

'I'm sorry about last week,' she said. 'I was being stupid. But please let's forget it. I've got so much to tell you.'

Roxana couldn't resist for long, and soon they were swapping stories and laughing together again.

'The cottages were filthy this week,' grumbled Roxana. 'You can't imagine the state of one of the bathrooms. Gross.'

'Worse than poo-picking,' said Kiri. And that was when the trouble started. Tanya had been sneaking about behind them and overheard the whole conversation. Soon the whole class was in hysterics over Kiri's new job. They held their noses whenever she came near them, and the mockery continued in class.

'Pick any theorem you like,' said the maths teacher to the class in general, 'and we'll relate it to problems in real life.' There was the usual silence, until Tanya piped up from the back, 'Kiri's good at picking,' and the whole room dissolved into laughter. Kiri's face was burning, but when the teacher took her aside later to ask if she was being bullied, she shook her head.

'I'm fine, thanks.'

It took all week for Tanya to get bored of the joke. Kiri had never been so glad to get to Friday, when she would have the added excitement of finding out about Ben. But when she got home, things didn't go to plan. Her father sent a text saying he'd be late and in place of his car, she was annoyed to see Steph's open-top parked outside the front door.

'Hello,' said Kiri in a tone of voice that meant goodbye.

'I hoped to find Jim in,' said Steph.

'He'll be back this evening. Not sure when.'

There was an awkward silence. Kiri knew she ought to offer Steph a cup of coffee, but she wanted her to go before her father got home. She felt defensive on his behalf. Steph had apparently walked out on him just because he hadn't got lots of money to spend on her any more. The words 'mean cow' hovered at the back of her mind.

'I'm sorry about Foxy,' said Steph. 'I heard he'd been sold, and I knew you'd be gutted.'

'I was. But there's nothing you can do about it.' Kiri couldn't keep the hostility out of her voice.

'You don't like me much, do you?' said Steph sadly. 'So I'd best be going. Tell Jim I called in. I came over for a couple of days for a business appointment and I'm flying back to New York tomorrow. But I'll be at my usual hotel tonight, if he wants to call me.'

She drove off, leaving Kiri feeling guilty, especially as it was only quarter of an hour before her father arrived home.

'Have you called the dog warden?' she asked as soon as he was sitting down at the kitchen table.

'Yes. And he's yours.'

Kiri threw her arms round his neck. 'Thank you, Dad. That's brilliant! Can Roxana come with us to fetch him and then have a sleepover with us?'

'Of course.'

When Kiri gave him the message from Steph, his face closed up.

'She said you could call her at the hotel.'

'I'll think about it.'

'She shouldn't have walked out on you like that.'

Her father looked up, puzzled. 'Whatever gave

you that idea? I was the one who decided to end our relationship. Steph wanted to put some of her money into my business but I couldn't have that. She's in the middle of divorcing a husband who took all her money, and the last thing she needs is another man teetering on the edge of bankruptcy. I can't get involved with her again until I'm back on my own two feet.'

Kiri felt terrible. She'd completely misunderstood the situation. Now she felt sorry for Steph and mean for not being friendlier.

When they picked up Roxana and went to the kennels the next morning, there was a long wait while forms were filled in and her father paid the warden a hundred pounds.

'I didn't know we'd have to pay so much,' said Kiri, wondering how many weekends of poo-picking it would take to pay the money back.

'It's a present,' said her father. 'Worth every penny to see a smile on your face again.'

The smile cracked wide open as Ben bounded into the warden's office and jumped up at Kiri with his tail wagging. She held his face in her hands and let him kiss her nose.

'You're crying!' accused Roxana.

'Only because I'm so happy.'

After a quick stop at the pet shop to buy a collar and lead, they went back to Walland Farm and gave

Ben his first lesson in coming when called. They let him loose at the end of a long rope in the small paddock and called his name. If he took no notice, they tugged on the rope until he came back and rewarded him with a small treat. If he came at once, without having to be reminded with the rope, he got two treats and a mountain of praise and cuddles. After several attempts, he got the message, and the treats, every time.

'Collies are quick learners,' said Kiri proudly.

Roxana had been rather quiet during the training session. At first, Kiri didn't like to ask the reason, but she had to leave soon for Torebridge.

'Is something the matter?'

'I just wish I could have a dog too, but they don't allow pets in the holiday park.'

Kiri reached out and squeezed her friend's hand. 'One day you'll have a dog, but right now we're going to share Ben. He loves you as well as me.'

Roxana managed a small smile that broadened when Kiri asked her to look after Ben for the afternoon. 'I'll throw balls for him, and then he can sit with me while I catch up with my homework.'

Kiri left for the stables. She hadn't called during the week because it was too soon for William to have arrived. Besides, she'd been afraid of hearing that he'd turned the idea down flat. Neither Aggie nor Jen was in sight, so she propped her bike against the wall and wandered into the yard. She was astounded to hear the most wonderful sound in the world: the 'good morning' whinny that she'd heard every day at Walland Farm for the past six years.

For a second, she stood frozen in disbelief. Then she was running across the yard and throwing her arms round Foxy's neck. He rubbed his head up and down her jacket, and made the soft whickering noise that he always made when she came back after being away at school. Inside her head, Kiri was whickering too. She went inside the stable and took off his rug to see whether he was well. His fiery coat glowed as if it had been polished, but she was shocked by the amount of weight he'd lost. He'd always been kept fit, but now he was rake thin.

'What have they done to you, Foxy?' Kiri saw a net stuffed with quality hay hanging on the wall uneaten. And when she looked in the manger, it was half full of horse pellets. 'Why aren't you eating?' She ran her hand down his back and found the muscles tense under the glowing skin. There was a grooming kit hanging from a nail outside the stable, so she took it down and started giving him a slow and gentle brush. His coat didn't need brushing, but she hoped the familiar strokes would make him relax enough to eat. After ten minutes, he gave a snort and moved across the box to the hay. At first, he just sniffed. Next he pulled a mouthful out of the net and rolled it between his teeth as if he'd forgotten how hay tasted. And then he gulped it down as if he hadn't eaten for weeks. Looking at his ribs, Kiri thought he probably hadn't. Even though she was now way behind with her work, she carried on brushing while he ate, afraid that if she stopped, he would too.

'Don't stop.' Jen was leaning over the stable door. 'This is the first time I've seen him eat properly since he arrived. And keeping my star client alive is much more important than mucking out.' After a quarter of an hour, Kiri reckoned Foxy was relaxed enough to carry on eating without her presence. She slipped out of his loose box and started carrying fresh straw to the next row of stables.

Jen came to help. 'Has he ever gone off his food before?'

'Never,' said Kiri.

'He was like this in the Ashford yard, they said, and he hasn't improved since he came here. I'm beginning to get worried.'

'Perhaps he's just tense from being shut up in his box for too long. How much time does he have grazing in the field every day?'

'None.'

'*None?* That's cruel!'

'Well, I must admit, I don't like keeping horses in all

the time, particularly not a sensitive horse like Foxfire.'
Jen bit her lower lip. 'But William is determined to
have it his way. He thinks it's too risky to let a valuable
horse roam free in a field. He's afraid of him getting
kicked by another horse or cutting himself on a fence.'

'Can't you just let him out to graze when William's
not around?'

'I can't go behind a client's back. But I'll have
another go at persuading him.'

After finishing the second row of stables, Kiri went
back to check on Foxy and found Jen tacking him up.
'Can I watch while you ride him?'

'Not me. William's due for a coaching session.' She
looked at her watch. 'About ten minutes ago.'

'And he has to have the horse saddled for him!' Kiri
could hardly believe anyone could be so lazy.

'If I make him feel like an important client, he's
more likely to respond to my suggestions.'

'Can I watch?'

'Better if you don't – at least not obviously. William
can be very prickly in front of an audience. But if you
start working on the row of stables nearest the arena,
you'll be able to see some of it.'

Kiri worked fast, clearing out the dirty beds and
bringing bales of new straw. It was good fresh straw.
Aggie had never stinted on the quality of feed and
bedding at Torebridge. It was one of the reasons why

she'd been making a loss. A squeal of brakes announced William's arrival and a minute later he walked into the yard. He was a good-looking boy, with blond hair, grey eyes and a tanned skin. He was a year or so younger than Eddie but taller and broader. He gave Jen a lopsided smile.

'Sorry I'm late.'

As soon as he rode Foxy into the arena, Kiri knew she was watching an expert. He sat deep in the saddle with his long legs wrapped round Foxy's flanks. His hands were light and still, allowing the head freedom, while his legs created the impulsion from the powerful hindquarters. When he asked for an extended trot, Kiri had never seen Foxy move with such power and grace. And the half pass – a dressage movement in which a horse glides diagonally across the arena – was like something out of a ballet. Her work forgotten, Kiri stared at a partnership beyond anything she'd dreamed of. Eddie was a good rider, but he'd never had the skill to produce dressage like this. And she wasn't even on the same planet. She suddenly doubted whether her plan to bring Foxy home would be the best thing for him. Perhaps he'd do better with a wonderful rider like William.

'I'd like to try him over some poles,' said William. 'See how he jumps.'

'Kiri! Please can you help make a jumping lane?'

asked Jen. They carried plastic jump supports into the arena and put up a line of poles at regular intervals, creating an exercise to make a horse precise with his jumping. William circled the arena and approached the jumping lane at a steady trot. Foxy's ears were pricked and his eyes locked on to the line of jumps, which he skipped over with evident enjoyment. Jen asked William to repeat the exercise several times, changing the height of the jumps and the distance between them.

'That's enough of that,' said William. 'Build me a proper jump.' He didn't seem to have heard of the word 'please'.

Kiri started putting up a jump known as a spread, as wide as it was high.

'Not too big,' said Jen. 'This is a new partnership and we need to build the horse's confidence slowly.'

'He's jumped much bigger than this!' said Kiri, without thinking.

'How do you know?' snapped William. 'You're paid to muck out stables. Not interfere with the training of an advanced event horse.'

Kiri opened her mouth to tell him just how much she knew about Foxy's jumping abilities when Jen cut in.

'William's right, Kiri. I'm the coach and you need to get on with the rest of your work. I'd like you to start clearing up Hawthorn Field.'

Kiri's face was burning as she strode out of the arena and started pushing the wheelbarrow towards a line of hawthorns in the distance. The field was as far away from the arena as it was possible to go and still be within the boundaries of Torebridge. Jen must have chosen it deliberately to get rid of her. William was more than prickly – he was horribly rude. And Jen had taken his side! Kiri didn't care how good a rider he was; he didn't deserve Foxy. Serve him right if she emptied the wheelbarrow over his flash car and walked out on the job for ever. Then he and Jen could come running for advice on how to handle Foxy.

Chapter 13

The sight of her mother's bike – an old-fashioned boneshaker with sit-up-and-beg handlebars and a large wicker basket in front – brought tears to Kiri's eyes. She'd often seen her mother setting out across the marsh with a basket full of paints and sketchbooks. Her father had got it out of the garden shed and was pumping up the tyres.

'Sylvia loved this old bike,' he said with a sad smile. 'I don't want it to go to waste. And when I get it cleaned up you can go cycling together.'

'It's for me?' Roxana's face lit up, but she looked quickly at Kiri. 'Are you sure you don't mind?' She knew Kiri was possessive about her mother's things.

'She'd want you to have it.' Kiri meant it – she felt sure that her mother would have liked her new friend, so fierce but so sensitive.

After a hurried breakfast and a cycling lesson on

the lawn, they set off down the track to Torebridge.

'I thought you wanted to stay away from there after William was so rude,' said Roxana.

'I did. But I can't leave Foxy there on his own.'

Kiri went in front, followed by a wobbly Roxana and an excited Ben. When they skidded on to the gravel in front of the bungalow, they found Aggie throwing balls for her terrier, Fiver. Ben dived into the game and stole the ball until Roxana made him give it back.

'This is my friend, Roxana,' said Kiri. 'I've brought her to see Foxy although she doesn't know much about horses.'

'But she's obviously good with dogs.' Aggie nodded at Roxana. 'She can take them both for a walk while you get on with your work.'

Kiri took Roxana to the row of loose boxes and was pleased when Foxy gave his welcoming whinny.

'He's beautiful,' said Roxana. 'Can I touch him?'

'Of course. He likes having his head rubbed. Like this.'

While Roxana left to walk the dogs, Kiri started mucking out the stables. She was still angry with Jen, and whenever she thought of William she stabbed the pitchfork so deep into the straw that she jarred her shoulder.

'When you've finished that row of boxes, come and help me in the arena.' Jen's voice was light and friendly, as if she didn't realize the anger she'd stoked.

Kiri took her time. The arena could stay unraked for all she cared. But when she finally made her way there, she found there was no raking to be done. Jen was lungeing a Welsh pony. A pretty grey with a sweet face, it was circling Jen obediently at the end of the lunge rope.

'Don't be taken in by Maisie's looks,' said Jen. 'That angelic face doesn't stop her bucking her young owner off.' As if on cue, the pony got to the end of the arena and kicked her heels in the air. 'I'm too heavy to ride her, but you're light enough to sort her out.'

Pleased to be asked to do something challenging, Kiri forgot to feel resentful about William. She rode Maisie in figures of eight, making her trot steadily and pushing her forward every time she felt the muscles in the pony's back bunching ready for a buck.

'Is that better?'

'Much. If you make her do as she's told on a regular basis, there's a good chance she'll behave well for her eight-year-old owner too.' Jen followed Kiri into Maisie's stable and watched her putting on a rug. 'You're a good rider, Kiri. You seem to have a knack of listening to horses but not letting them get too cheeky. I'll try and give you some more rides like that.'

'Can I ride Foxy?'

'No!' Jen's voice barked in exasperation. 'I know it's

hard, but you have to stay away from Foxy and not interfere in the coaching sessions. The relationship between rider and coach is special, as you'll find out one day for yourself. I can't have you butting in.'

'Not even if I have something useful to say?'

'Especially not then. Like I said, William's a touchy customer, and more so now that I've told him Foxy belonged to your brother. If you want to go on working here, you've got to keep quiet for both our sakes. I need to keep William as a top client, and you want to go on looking after his horse. I warned you it would be difficult.'

Kiri agreed reluctantly. 'Is Foxy eating better?' she asked.

'Yes. William's allowing him to go out every day, and I've got you to thank for that.'

Later that day, William came to ride accompanied by his father, Grant, who watched stony faced as William gave an elegant display of Foxy's paces in the arena. Without a word of praise for his son's dressage skills, he asked to see the horse jump. As soon as Jen put up a good-sized fence, Kiri noticed how William's hands tensed. Foxy rolled the top pole on to the ground.

'Careless,' said Grant. 'You'll need to do better than that if I'm to go on spending all this money on your eventing career.'

William scowled as he got off, and Kiri almost

sympathized. A father like that would make anyone rude; no wonder William was so difficult.

When her work was finished, Kiri found Roxana in the bungalow.

'Your friend's been reading to me,' said Aggie. 'My eyes aren't what they were, and it's been a great pleasure. You'll come again next week, won't you?'

'She paid me to read!' said Roxana as they cycled away. 'Not a lot. But I'd much rather read than clean.'

Kiri set out for home by a different route.

'Why this way?'

'I want to show you one of Mum's favourite places.'

They sprinted along the dykes with their hair flying out in the wind and Ben barking at their heels, until they turned a corner and there it was: a small, ancient church stranded on the marsh in the middle of nowhere. Sheep grazed right up to walls surrounded by a jigsaw of ditches.

'How did people get here?' asked Roxana.

'On foot, I suppose, or on a horse. Mum liked it because of what she called the ghosts: people from the surrounding villages who disappeared. She did a painting of how it might have looked.'

'What else did she paint?'

'The marsh mostly, but not just the pretty bits. She liked painting ugly things too, like the pylons and the power station at Dungeness.'

Ben was whining for his supper, so they pedalled back to Walland Farm, where Jim had built a good fire in the sitting room. 'I've got another surprise for you,' he said, leading the way up to Kiri's bedroom. She opened the door and took a deep breath. The elegant daybed with blue painted ironwork from her mother's studio had been brought upstairs and covered with an Indian bedspread.

'It's a sofa for you and a bed for Roxana when she's here.'

'It's lovely,' said Roxana. 'But won't you want to sleep in it, Kiri, as it was your mother's?'

'No, it's for you.' Kiri was surprised to find she didn't mind. She'd been afraid of going into the studio ever since the funeral. Too many painful visions of her mother standing in front of the easel or curled up on the daybed with a book. Yet now it was in her room, the bed kept its memories but had a new life of its own.

After dinner, Kiri's father left for Liverpool, and Marina came to spend the night at Walland Farm. The two girls took Ben upstairs and talked until midnight.

'I can keep an eye on Foxy, but I've got to do more than that. I want to bring him back to Walland Farm.'

'How much would he cost to buy?'

'Thousands. If William would sell him.'

'We'll win the lottery and make him an offer too big to resist.'

'Or we could discover treasure in the lost villages.'

'If we had a metal detector.'

Roxana fell asleep, but Kiri's head was whirling with unlikely plans for getting rich. The small amount of cash she earned at the stables was never going to buy a valuable event horse, and she couldn't ask her father for money. There'd been deep worry lines round his eyes as he set out for Liverpool. Perhaps Eddie would win a big race and solve all their problems. And pigs would fly. Deep down, Kiri was certain that Foxy's future was up to her alone. She leant over the edge of the bed and patted Ben, who thumped his tail on the carpet.

'I rescued you against all the odds. Now you and I have got to do the same for Foxy.'

Chapter 14

It wasn't Kiri's fault that William ended up in hospital. After Jen asked her to stay away from William's coaching sessions, she'd made herself scarce whenever he turned up. She went to check the fields at the far end of Torebridge or took Maisie out for a hack. The pony's rider and her mother had been delighted with the progress Kiri had made, and were paying her to school or hack out twice a week.

'I told you,' said Jen. 'You have this ability to connect with animals. Maisie's become a different pony since you started riding her.'

Kiri was getting other rides too. She occasionally took Greyling out to stop his joints becoming too stiff, and another woman had asked her to teach a young horse how to jump. Kiri wondered if she could one day become a coach like Jen, but first she'd have to make her name as a successful rider in the eventing world.

And how could that happen to someone who didn't even have a horse of her own?

The trouble started at half-term when the girls came to the stables every day, Kiri to work in the yard, and Roxana to help Aggie with dog walking or reading. William also had a week off from the sixth form college where he was studying for his international baccalaureate. For most of the week, he concentrated on flatwork – preparation for dressage – and Kiri, getting occasional glimpses from a distance, was again stunned by the way Foxy responded to a truly skilled rider.

At the end of the week, William decided to focus on jumping and asked Kiri to build the jumps. 'There's no need for you to lug heavy jumps around,' he told Jen with a smile. Kiri suspected he had another motive besides saving Jen some work. He no doubt wanted to show off how much better Foxy was at jumping now. She carried the jump uprights and poles into the arena where Jen asked her to set up a triple, consisting of two small jumps and a big spread. The idea was that the smaller jumps would ensure that the horse reached the big one on the right stride. All went well for several circuits and William now had an audience including Aggie and Roxana, who'd come out to see the yard's star rider perform.

William said he wanted the small jumps removed, and, after getting a nod from Jen, Kiri did as he asked.

He approached the single obstacle in the same rhythm, but his hands were tense and Foxy cat-leapt the fence, throwing William on to the pommel. The next time, William rushed the approach and two poles fell to the ground.

'Careless brute!' said William and hit Foxy hard on the shoulder with his whip. Foxy had never been treated like this before. His ears flattened and his neck foamed with sweat.

'Let's take a break,' said Jen, but William wasn't listening. On the third attempt, he galloped even faster at the fence and when Foxy stopped dead, he picked up the whip and thrashed him hard on the hindquarters. Kiri felt the pain as if she was being beaten herself. She looked into Foxy's panicked eyes and knew she had to act. Her hand closed on the clicker device in her pocket – she'd been using it to train Ben that morning – and clicked. An arc of understanding flashed between her and Foxy, who reared up in the classical levade, sending William tumbling backwards on to the sand.

'Well done, Foxy,' said Kiri under her breath. 'William's got to have the sense to stop now.'

But he didn't. Unhurt except for the blow to his dignity, William got straight back on and rode angrily towards the jump. But Foxy had had enough. Having learned from Kiri's clicker that he could get rid of a rider he didn't like, he cleared the jump, gave a wild buck and galloped straight for the barrier surrounding the arena. Kiri's heart stopped. The barrier was too high. But Foxy gathered himself together and, with a stupendous effort, cleared the top rail. Without William. Already unbalanced by the buck, he was unseated by the huge bound and fell to the ground with a bone-crunching thud. Everything went into slow motion: Jen running to William's side, Aggie phoning for an ambulance, Foxy swerving through the stable gates and galloping into the distance.

Kiri ran to see if she could help. William was unconscious, and his arm lay at an odd angle. Jen was checking his breathing and pulse, while Aggie gave directions to the emergency service, and Roxana hurried to get a blanket from the house.

'I can look after him till the ambulance arrives,' said Jen. 'Nothing more you can do here, so go after Foxy.'

Kiri dashed out of the farm with Ben beside her and followed the hoof prints leading out on to the marsh. Foxy was a long way ahead and, although he was no longer galloping, the steady beat of his hooves told her he wasn't in a mood to stop and wait. It might be a long chase. She set out with the loping stride she'd learned in cross-country races at her last school. She could keep the pace up for miles, and if she lost the trail, Ben would show her the way to go.

The hoof prints followed the top of a dyke for a

more than a mile and then stopped. Ben was hunting around for a scent when Kiri spotted a mark at the bottom of the bank. She scrambled down to have a look and saw that Foxy had jumped off the edge of the dyke and doubled back behind a line of scrubby hawthorns. What was he doing? And then she knew. He was on his way home to Walland Farm. Her heart ached at the thought of him bolting to safety in the place where he'd always been loved. What was she going to do when she found him? Send him back to William? She ran faster, hoping to catch him before he reached the sanctuary of his old stall in the barn. It would be heartbreaking to have to drag him out of there. In the end, she found him standing on the path outside Walland Farm. He was leaning over the fence nuzzling gently at his old friend, Mouse.

Kiri pressed her face against Foxy's neck and cried. It was horrible to have to send him back, but there was no alternative. If she tried to hide him in the barn, he'd be found immediately and she'd never be allowed to see him again. She knotted the broken reins and mounted. It would be a long, sad ride back to Torebridge.

Soon the winter sun was dropping to the horizon and its blood-red rays turned the ditches into rivers of fire. A swan glided along the water beside the bridleway, and a moorhen darted into the reeds with a croak of alarm. Suddenly Ben growled. Foxy refused to move forward. Kiri peered into the gloom to see what had startled them and saw a small body shuffling across the path. A badger! She saw the flash of its striped face as it turned to look at them before scuttling into the undergrowth. The marsh was at its most magical on a winter's evening, and she longed to stay out there with Foxy for ever. They passed one of the small brick shelters built hundreds of years ago for the 'lookers' – shepherds who looked after the Romney Marsh flocks – and Kiri imagined leading Foxy and Ben inside. There would be just enough space for the three of them to bed down for the night. How she wished she could fall asleep to the sound of hay being munched and the scrape of a hoof on bare earth.

It was nearly dark when she reached the stables. Aggie was waiting for her at the gate.

'We were worried about you.'

'How's William?' asked Kiri as she unsaddled Foxy and rugged him up against the chill of the night.

'He came round soon after you left, thank God. And Jen rang from the hospital. They think it's only a mild concussion. He's got a broken arm, but it'll mend.'

'And Foxy's not hurt. I checked him over as soon as I found him.'

'William got off lightly – he could have been killed. He should have listened to his coach.'

Marina took Roxana home. Aggie had already

phoned Jim McFarlane. When he arrived at the stable yard, he gave Kiri one of his bear hugs.

'Thank goodness it wasn't you who got hurt!' He was reassured to hear William had suffered nothing more serious than a broken arm. 'Although that's bad enough. I expect Grant Harding will call me to complain.'

'It wasn't Foxy's fault,' said Kiri, burning with indignation. William beat him really hard.'

'The main thing is that you'll soon be home safe and sound. I had nightmares about you getting lost on the marsh.'

'Never. And certainly not with Foxy and Ben. They'll always look after me.'

That night Kiri fell asleep wondering what would happen to Foxy while William was recovering. She dreamed of snuggling up with him and Ben in a lookers' hut.

Something clicked inside Foxy's brain. Last night, when she'd ridden him away from his old home, he'd felt a wave of misery echoed by the sadness in his rider. He obeyed her legs, which urged him forward, but he knew her heart wanted them to turn back. In the morning, a sense of resignation replaced the restlessness he'd felt before. This was his home now. It wasn't his choice and that new rider wasn't to be trusted – he could be cruel. But she was there some of the time. It would have to do.

Chapter 15

'William will be off riding for eight weeks,' said Jen. 'And of course you're desperate to know what the plans are for Foxy.'

Kiri nodded. She was afraid that Foxy might be taken to a different yard.

'Don't worry. He's to stay here and I'm to train him for Downlands, the event that qualifies riders for the eighteen and under National Championship.'

'That's at Easter, isn't it?'

'Yes. William's still hoping to ride in it but his doctor is less optimistic.'

'Will Foxy be ready for it?'

'Only if I can restore his confidence in jumping. And I've got to get Tanker ready as well for the open event on the same day.'

Kiri offered to help in any way she could. She knew Jen wouldn't let her ride Foxy without getting permission from William, but perhaps she could help get Tanker fit by lungeing him in the schooling arena. To her surprise, once Jen was satisfied that she could control Tanker, she took over all his fitness work including interval training, which consisted of short bursts – or intervals – of fast work alternating with a steady walk. The first interval was a six-minute canter and Kiri was amazed to discover how long that felt. She was glad of the strength she'd acquired from cross-country running and cycling.

Kiri's help allowed Jen to concentrate on Foxy. She was good at dressage and had him dancing through the sequence of movements in the dressage test scheduled for Downlands. She was also an experienced showjumper, but she couldn't find the key to restoring his confidence over jumps. A cross-country practice was out of the question until he was happy going over the poles in the arena, but every time he approached the line of jumps, his ears went flat, and she could feel him searching for a way to get her off. He didn't succeed, but this was no way to prepare for a big event.

'I'm going to turn him out in the field for a few days and see if that does the trick,' she told Kiri. 'Give him a chance to relax.'

The following weekend, when Jen had gone to see her sister, Kiri went straight to the paddock where Foxy was resting. She rubbed his nose, scratched him behind the ears and took his rug off, so she could see how he was looking. He was beginning to fill out, and she stood back to admire the bright chestnut coat rippling over muscles that had grown stronger with all the schooling. He started following her as if she were leader of the herd. It felt as though they were back home at Walland Farm and suddenly, almost without thinking, she reached up and pulled herself on to his back. Just like before, she used her voice and her weight to steer him round the paddock. She refused to feel guilty. This wasn't real riding – it was just her and Foxy being together again. He flicked his tail with pleasure and broke into a gentle trot. As they came round the corner his ears pricked at the sight of a fallen log and before she knew it, they popped over.

'What the hell are you doing!' Jen had got back early and had walked up to the top paddock.

'Sorry. I didn't set out to jump him – it just sort of happened.' Kiri jumped off guiltily, and Foxy followed her to the five-barred gate on which Jen was leaning with a thoughtful look in her eyes.

'Am I going mad or did I just see you jump that horse without a saddle or bridle?'

'Sorry. I would never have ridden him properly without asking permission, but this was just a bit of fun.'

'Have you done it before?'

111

'Not here,' said Kiri quickly. 'But I often rode him like that at home.' She went to pick up his rug and when she came back with it, Jen tilted her head to one side.

'I've got an idea. Tack him up and bring him to the arena.'

Kiri did as she asked and watched while Jen trotted him in circles. As usual, he was going beautifully for her, but instead of carrying on, she got off and handed the reins to Kiri.

'Trot a figure of eight and then turn him into the jumping lane. Don't make a big deal of it – just ride like you did bareback in the field.'

This was the first time Kiri had been asked to ride Foxy at Torebridge. Although she sensed this was a turning point for all of them, she refused to let her body grow tense. She sat lightly in the saddle and guided Foxy loosely towards the first pole. His ears flicked forward, and she felt him focus on the line of jumps ahead. He skipped over the first three and, without changing pace, sailed over the big spread at the end. She went round again with the same, perfect result. Jen raised and widened the jump. It was bigger than anything Kiri had ever attempted, but she put her trust in Foxy. He responded with a huge leap that left every pole still in place.

'Now try it without the striding poles,' said Jen.

'Just imagine they're still there.' This was going to be really hard. Kiri took a deep breath and stifled the urge to say she couldn't do it. Couldn't risk damaging Foxy's confidence all over again.

'You'll be fine.' Jen had guessed how she was feeling. Kiri took an even deeper breath and rode straight and steady towards the spread. One, two, three strides and he met the fence perfectly, surging into the air as if he had wings.

'My hunch was right,' said Jen. 'He'll only jump when he trusts his rider. That's why it went so wrong with William. And although he trusts me a little, you're the one who can really inspire him.'

Kiri glowed inside at the compliment. 'But William will never let me train Foxy for him.'

'We'll see. He wants to ride in the Downlands event, and if I'll tell him you're the only person who can get Foxy jumping well enough for that, he might agree.'

Roxana was bubbling with excitement as they cycled back to Walland Farm. 'You were brilliant. Aggie and I were watching from inside the bungalow and she says you've got natural talent.'

Kiri blushed. 'Foxy and I just understand each other – that's all.'

'You never give yourself enough credit. Like in maths. You could be top every week, if you wanted to.'

Kiri's thoughts were tumbling over each other. The Easter holidays started in a couple of weeks' time. And if William agreed, she could ride Foxy every day: interval training in the big field, hacking out on the marsh, bounding over the jumps. But it was a big 'if'.

'William doesn't like me. So he'll probably say no, out of spite.'

'But he does like Jen,' said Roxana. 'You may not have noticed the way he looks at her, but I have. He came to Torebridge for Jen. So if she says you're to ride Foxy, you will.'

Chapter 16

The next few weeks passed in a haze of excitement for Kiri. Roxana had been right about William doing whatever Jen wanted. He agreed that Kiri could jump Foxy so long as Jen trained him on the flat.

'I'm not having Kiri ruin his dressage,' he'd said, according to Aggie. 'And I'm not paying her. If she's that soppy about the horse, she can do it for love.'

The days were getting longer and Kiri spent every moment of her free time at the stables. As well as riding Foxy, she had to do the mucking out she was paid to do and she couldn't abandon Maisie.

'I won't stop getting Tanker fit either,' said Kiri. But Jen was firm.

'You can't do everything. And if you're doing most of the work with Foxy, I can manage Tanker myself.'

Training for the same deadline, Jen and Kiri often took the horses out together. Jen believed in working them on the beach. The long hack across the marsh to Camber was good for their legs, and interval training on the sand gave them the stamina they'd need in the cross-country phase of the event. Splashing through the waves, Kiri couldn't believe how far she'd come since the mad gallop on Christmas Day. She now found it easy to balance Foxy in canter even with the distraction of Tanker fighting to get ahead alongside. Ben often came with them, dashing in and out of the waves and barking at the windsurfers.

The horses needed hill work too. Once a week, Jen insisted on loading them into her horsebox and driving them on to the South Downs. Kiri loved riding up there. It was like travelling along the roof ridge of the world. On one side, she looked down on the shifting colours of the sea. On the other, a mosaic of woods and fields stretched far into the Weald, once a vast and dangerous forest. People had travelled the Downs for thousands of years and when Foxy shied at a burial mound, Kiri thought of ancient spirits jealously guarding their treasure.

'I wish I could discover a treasure trove and have enough money to buy Foxy,' she said wistfully.

Jen gave her a sympathetic smile. 'Believe me, I know how you feel. I had a horse once that I trained to advanced level, but I had to sell him to make ends meet.'

'How awful!'

'It was. But he went to a good home. My advice is to live in the present, like now, with the sun shining on the Downs and two wonderful horses to ride.'

She laughed as she kicked Tanker on and they galloped up the hill side by side.

They were there to train as well as enjoy the ride. Jen explained that the cross-country course at Downlands was hilly, and Foxy had to learn to keep cantering whatever the gradient. She showed Kiri how to lean forward but keep her legs driving the horse on as they bounded up a steep slope. Going downhill in canter was terrifying. Kiri looked down the hill they'd just come up and felt dizzy. At first, she hung on to Foxy's mouth so much that he came to a halt. But the more she practised, the more she discovered the knack of keeping a regular canter, up- and downhill.

The next step – a big one – was to take Foxy on a cross-country practice.

'Cross-country is the heart of eventing,' said Jen, her face lighting up at the thought of doing the thing she loved best. 'The dressage and showjumping are important, but the reason why people love eventing is the chance to gallop across open country, jumping scary fences. It gives you a high like no other.'

Kiri had done a bit of cross-country with Mouse, but it was a long time ago and she was worried she might let Foxy down.

'That's why we're going on a practice at a place with a huge variety of obstacles,' said Jen. 'It'll give you the confidence to face anything.'

As soon as they came out of the horsebox, the horses sensed they were somewhere exciting. Tanker waltzed round Jen while she tacked him up, and Foxy pawed at the ground as Kiri tightened his girth.

They started with a line of brush fences like the ones built for steeplechase races. Tanker went first but Kiri wasn't ready for what the adrenalin of cross-country would do to Foxy. He shot away like a bullet from a gun and galloped flat out over the first two fences before she got hold of him. They went on to jump hedges, gates, barrels and banks. Once or twice Foxy hesitated, but Kiri kept her legs on – not kicking but squeezing his flanks to urge him forward – and they got over safely, if not elegantly.

'Now for the water,' said Jen. 'You don't want an event horse to have any hang-ups about water or ditches.' She led the way to a big complex of water jumps. There were options for an easy trot in and out of the water, a jump down into it from a bank, and a brush fence, which was so high that the horse had to jump blind – without seeing that it was going to land in water until it had already taken off.

'You go first,' said Jen.

Although Kiri was used to water because she'd

had a lot of practice jumping ditches at Walland Farm, she'd never seen anything like this. Her heart pounded as she got Foxy going in the strong, bouncy canter that was the best way to approach water. Jen hadn't said which route to choose, and she didn't want to be a wimp, so she gritted her teeth and headed for the big brush. Foxy was keen – just as well when Kiri realized the size of the jump they were approaching. She sat back, urged him forward with her legs and kicked hard on take-off just to make sure. They sailed into the air, and when she looked down at the water glinting below it felt like slow motion, until they landed with a huge splash. Foxy didn't even peck on landing. He gathered himself together and bounded up a one-metre bank on the far side of the water. She gave him a big pat on the neck and looked round for Jen, who joined her looking pale.

'Do you realize what you did? You've just come through the advanced water jump – the sort of obstacle they have at Badminton. I assumed you'd take the novice route.'

When Kiri looked back at the fence they'd cleared, she could hardly believe it herself.

'We're nearly done,' said Jen. 'But before we leave, we need to show Foxy a "skinny". This was a type of fence Kiri had never seen before – a fence so narrow that it almost invited a horse to get penalties for a run-out. The one Jen chose was a brush fence, less than a metre wide.

'Hold him steady until the last moment, or he'll nip out the side door.' Jen demonstrated with Tanker and made it look easy. Kiri tried to copy her but gave Foxy his head too soon and he slid along the side of the jump. The next time he did the same in the other direction, and the third time Kiri shot over his shoulder on to the ground. She didn't hurt herself, but she was worried that she was teaching Foxy bad habits.

'Try once more,' said Jen, 'and imagine you're riding him though a narrow gap where you don't want to catch your knees on the sides.'

Kiri thought of the gap between the barn and the gatepost at Walland Farm and Foxy got the message, jumping neatly through. She did it twice more and felt like a professional.

'That was the most exciting thing I've *ever* done,' Kiri said as they washed the sweat off the steaming horses. 'I can't believe I jumped that skinny!'

'And an advanced water jump,' said Jen, shaking her head.

'Foxy looks after me.'

'He does. And you're a better rider than you think you are. You're a natural.'

Kiri was so elated that nothing could puncture the balloon of her happiness – not even the sight of William's frowning face when they got back to Torebridge.

'My doctor has forbidden me to ride at Downlands,' he said as they unloaded the horses. 'Too risky in case I fall on my arm before it's completely healed.'

'I'm sorry. You'd better withdraw straight away,' said Jen.

Kiri sighed. She'd loved getting Foxy ready for the event and she'd been sure he'd do well.

'I don't want to withdraw. Foxy needs all the experience he can get if he and I are to be noticed by the selectors for Britain's Young Rider team. I was hoping you'd ride him for me.'

'Impossible. I can't ride in the Under Eighteen class and all the other sections are full.'

'Damn.'

'You could put Kiri in as a substitute rider in the Under Eighteen.'

'Kiri!'

'She's just had a brilliant cross-country practice – she and Foxy jumped the advanced water.'

'They'd be a laughing stock in the dressage.'

'The selectors already know how well you ride a dressage test – so that's not an issue.'

'Mmm.'

'Come inside and we can talk about it over a cup of coffee while Kiri puts the horses away.'

Kiri's hands were shaking as she changed the

horses' rugs. It was cruel to have such a dream dangled in front of her only to have it snatched away because of her lack of experience in dressage. She lingered in the stables with Foxy and Tanker, dreading the moment when William would pronounce the final 'no'.

At long last, Jen emerged from the bungalow with her arm round William's shoulders.

'I'm really sorry you can't ride yourself at Downlands, but you've made the right decision.' Turning to Kiri, she smiled. 'It's settled. If your father approves, you'll take William's place at Downlands.'

Kiri was too amazed to speak. She couldn't imagine what magic Jen had used to get William's agreement.

'I expect my father will pay your registration and entry fees,' said William, 'but he'll never agree to pay you for training Foxy.' He looked embarrassed. 'Sorry – I know you're hard up.'

Kiri was still too shocked to say anything more than a whispered thank you.

As William walked back to his father's car, Kiri's heart was singing at the thought of riding Foxy in an event. Nearer the time, she'd be terrified, but right now she was floating on air.

'How did you make him give me the ride?' she asked Jen, as soon as William had left.

'I didn't "make" him do anything. He knows Foxy will jump for you.'

Kiri hurried home to give Roxana and her father the good news. Her father asked parent-like questions about safety and money, but he seemed happy with the answers. Roxana was thrilled, and Kiri told her about the cross-country practice over and over again – until she saw a glazed look come into her friend's eyes.

'Sorry. I'm being a bore. You tell me what dream *you'd* like to come true.'

Roxana wrinkled her nose as if she didn't have many dreams. 'I love horses, but I'm afraid of big ones like Foxy. Do you think I could sit on Mouse?'

'Of course you can!' Kiri wanted to kick herself for not thinking of it before. 'He's retired, but he can still carry you round the paddock. You're not nearly as tall as me.'

They went to find Mouse, and Kiri showed Roxana how to mount. She let the stirrup down to make it easier and gave a helping hand as Roxana wobbled her way on to the saddle. 'That's how you hold the reins. Now tap his sides with your heels.'

Kiri put her hand on the reins and between them they persuaded Mouse to walk slowly round the edge of the field. A big grin appeared on Roxana's face as she got off and gave Mouse a kiss.

'You can ride him whenever you like.'

Ben came up to them, wagging his tail. They couldn't go up to the hayloft because the ladder wasn't dog friendly, so Kiri took them to a brick building on the other side of the farmhouse. 'Dad started to convert this into a holiday cottage but it never got finished. Eddie and I turned one of the rooms into a den, which we used to pretend was a lookers' hut.' Kiri showed Roxana the room, which had a fireplace, a table and two chairs. There were rushes on the stone floor and bunches of lavender hanging on the walls.

'Tell me more about your family,' said Kiri as they shared a packet of biscuits with Ben.

'Not much to tell: my father disappeared soon after I was born, I don't remember him. My great-grandma and cousins came to England with us; they live in Lydd.'

'What's your great-grandma like?'

'She's an old school Roma. She wears long, embroidered skirts and shawls and her fingers are covered in rings.'

'I'd like to meet her and have my fortune told.'

Roxana rolled her eyes. 'You might not like what she tells you.'

Chapter 17

The rest of the month speeded up until Kiri found herself grooming and plaiting Foxy on the day of the Downlands event. Because Foxy had the long flowing mane of his 'Luso' sire, Jen told her to do an Andalusian braid, which gathered all the hair into a thick plait along the crest of his neck. It was quite different from the line of eleven separate plaits on Tanker. Kiri stood back and admired her work. Foxy looked beautiful.

Jen drove them to Downlands where they left the horses in the box while they went to inspect the course.

'You have to walk the course from the point of view of your horse,' explained Jen. 'Look out for things that could spook him.' She was already walking briskly to the first jump, an inviting brush fence. In fact, the first five jumps were straightforward, or so Kiri thought.

'This one looks easy, but it's not.' Jen was pointing at some rails on the edge of a wood. 'It's called a tiger trap, but it'll catch a few humans later today. The horses will be jumping from bright daylight into a dark wood and they won't be able to see what's there – as far as they know there could be a ten-foot drop or a real tiger. So Foxy will have to trust you.'

Kiri knew she was lucky to have an expert guide. On her own, she wouldn't have given that fence a second look. After a couple more obstacles, they came to the water jump, which looked almost as hard as the one at the practice, but Jen assured her it wasn't. Next the course went up the side of the Downs, and Kiri was glad of all the practice she'd had at balancing a horse on steep slopes. The uphill jumps didn't look too bad but the one at the top was terrifying.

'It looks like a ski jump,' said Kiri, 'launching you into space.' The ground where a horse would land was a long way down. She wondered if it would be OK to close her eyes on take-off.

'You'll be fine, and you can hail a taxi if you like.' Jen grinned at Kiri's puzzled expression. 'That's equestrian slang for flinging up an arm to keep your balance.' She skipped down the slope to the next fence. 'This is the one you *do* need to worry about.' It was a 'skinny', strategically placed so that riders who landed badly after the ski jump would almost certainly have a run-out.

The rest of the course blurred into a whirl of

spreads, ditches, hedges and gates. Kiri's mind was a cocktail of excitement and terror – not of falling but of letting Foxy down.

Just as they were tacking up Foxy, Kiri's father called her mobile to say he wasn't going to make it to Downlands after all. Kiri hovered between feeling disappointed that he wasn't coming and relieved that he wouldn't be there to witness a disaster. If there was one.

'That's OK, Dad. I've got Jen to look after me and Marina's going to bring Roxana and Aggie to watch the cross-country.'

'Call me as soon as you've finished.'

The sight of the arena where Foxy's dressage test was due to start in half an hour let loose a rabble of butterflies inside Kiri's stomach. Jen helped her find her competitor's number and made sure she had the right clothes, including a black jacket borrowed from a client at the stables. But then she had to leave to get Tanker ready for his dressage.

'You'll be fine,' said Jen. 'Keep Foxy moving so he doesn't start messing about. Remember it's his first event too and he probably feels as nervous as you do.'

Foxy pawed the ground so Kiri urged him forward and started practising some of the movements in the test. It seemed to be going well until she saw William and his father approaching with a tall, grey-haired woman.

'This is the horse,' said William, without any introductions. 'With the right rider, he could do a really good test.'

'I'm Marianne Jackson, your Under Eighteen Regional Representative,' said the woman. 'I see from the programme that you're Kiri McFarlane.'

Kiri nodded. Foxy felt as if he was about to explode with excitement and she wanted to get him away but didn't like to say so. Luckily Mrs Jackson spotted the problem.

'Don't feel you have to stay here talking if you need to work him in.'

Kiri moved off and almost immediately the steward told her to start trotting round the outside of the arena. 'The judge will sound her car horn when she's ready for you to start.'

The horn blared out, sending Foxy plunging towards the entrance. Kiri sat back in the saddle and prayed. If they started the test like this, she'd come bottom for sure. She turned Foxy in a tight circle to get his attention and then they were in. They trotted much too fast up the centre line and Kiri was late with her aid to tell Foxy to turn right in front of the judge. For one horrible moment she thought he was going to stumble over the white board at the end of the arena and crash into the judge's car.

'Get a grip!' she told herself and started riding more

assertively. She slowed the trot and managed a good strike off into canter. Foxy still felt like an unexploded bomb, but they were completing all the movements and she hadn't taken a wrong turning. They swung back on to the centre line at the end of the test and he did a beautiful halt, straight and square. As Kiri bowed to the judge, she hoped everyone would remember the halt at the end and not the entry.

She left the arena expecting to see the Hardings, but they'd disappeared. Had her test been that bad? She rode Foxy back to the horsebox and started getting him ready for the showjumping. It took longer than she expected and when she made her way to the show ring, there was already a long queue for the practice jump.

At last, Jen appeared. 'Sorry I wasn't here to help you earlier. How did the dressage go?

'Awful at the beginning. A bit better at the end.'

'What did William say?'

'He walked off, so it must have been dreadful.'

'I don't suppose it was that bad. And he should be here, helping you with the practice jump.'

Jen moved firmly in front of another rider's coach, explaining that they needed the fence because Foxy was due to go in. Even so, there was only time for one jump before their number was called.

As she entered the ring, Foxy gave an enormous buck, telling Kiri that the fuse to that unexploded bomb was getting shorter. Determined not to let him rush, she held him back too much and almost stopped at the first fence. A sharp kick got him over but launched him into a gallop, which only just left the next one standing. She had to take charge to avoid a total disaster. She sat up, held firmly on to the reins, and pushed him in a steady canter towards a spread. He cleared it by half a metre and snorted as if to ask why she hadn't ridden him properly before. They cleared several jumps on a curve and straightened for an upright, which had already been the downfall of a lot of riders. Safely over, Kiri took a deep breath and steadied for the wall, a double and the final fence.

She left the ring with a huge smile – only to have it wiped off her face by a frown from William, who'd arrived with his father and Marianne Jackson.

'The first two jumps were awful,' he said.

'But you recovered well,' said Marianne. 'And you went clear!'

William's father was muttering about the price he'd paid for Foxfire.

Jen hustled her away. 'Take no notice of them, especially William. He's frustrated because he wants to be riding here himself.'

After leaving Foxy back at the horsebox, Jen had to drag her to the results board.

'I don't want to know I'm bottom.'

'You won't be. There weren't many clears in the showjumping.'

At first when Kiri looked at the scores, she was confused. She got forty-two for her dressage, which didn't sound good. The person who'd done the test before her got fifty-seven.

'I told you I was hopeless.'

'Don't be silly. The scoring in eventing is based on penalty points so the lower the better.' With most of the dressage scores now up, Jen worked out that Foxy was placed in the middle of the Under Eighteen class. 'That's good for your first event, and you'll go up the order after all the showjumping results are in.'

Kiri was riding an emotional roller coaster. Saved from the disgrace of coming last, she was now poised on a wave of hope.

They went to look at Tanker's score. He was almost bottom of his class but Jen just laughed. 'That's Tanker for you – a jumping machine that refuses to do dressage.'

Nerves were making Kiri feel sick as she got ready for the cross-country. Foxy looked magnificent. She wished her own gear could do him justice, but she was all too conscious that she looked like someone dressed out of a charity shop. The other riders had state-of-the-art body protectors, cross-country shirts and helmet covers in matching colours, while she only had an old sweatshirt and Jen's rather battered body protector.

She'd spent some of the money she'd earned on riding boots, but she couldn't afford leather.

'What's the most important thing on the cross-country?' asked Jen as she walked beside Foxy towards the start.'

'I don't know.' Kiri felt ignorant as well as terrified.

'To have fun!'

They arrived at the start, where Foxy jigged about like a two year old. He was foaming with sweat and refused to go into the start box. Disgrace loomed when the official in charge looked at his watch and warned they'd be eliminated if they weren't inside the box within a minute. The Hardings were offering loud advice and Kiri felt like screaming in frustration. They needed to understand it from Foxy's point of view. He was only panicking because of all the emotion he sensed from everyone around him.

'Let go, Jen,' she said, and let the reins hang loose as she turned Foxy away from the box. Riding as if she were bridle free at home, she walked him round for half a minute before using her knees to nudge him through the gap into the box. She sat there with the reins still loose until the official finished the countdown.

'Three, two, one, go!' As she gathered up the reins, Foxy bucked, throwing her sideways out of the saddle. She managed to hang on, but found herself galloping towards the first fence of her first event having lost both her stirrups. The thought of falling off in front of William and his father made her lock her legs round Foxy like a vice. Her bareback riding paid off and they flew over together. By the third jump she'd got her feet back in the stirrups and when they reached the tiger trap into the dark, she was in control. Imagining the black hole that was all Foxy would see, she rode the fence as if it was the biggest one on the course. She felt him hesitate, kicked hard and he went.

'Good boy,' she said, leaning forward to pat his neck. The fences were coming up fast and she was in and out of the water before she had time to think. Next came the steep section, and she felt the power of the Lusitano in Foxy as he bounded up the hill. The big test was now ahead of her. She turned towards the ski jump and summoned all her courage. Because Foxy couldn't see his landing, he had to trust her and she used her whole body and mind to urge him forward. She blinked her eyes shut, so that they shared the leap into the unknown, and together they flew into the air. It was a long way down but now Foxy's natural agility came to his aid. He landed like a cat and a touch from the reins guided him neatly through the skinny.

With the hardest fence over, Kiri let the exhilaration rip. She was grinning as they leapt gates and walls and splashed through the second water. Foxy flew towards the last jump, which was built to look like a dog kennel.

She sensed him roll his eyes at a painted spaniel but nothing would stop them now. They were clear! She jumped off and threw her arms round Foxy's neck.

'Brilliant!' Jen had listened to Kiri's progress on the loudspeaker system and thumped her on the back.

'Well done,' said William, who'd come to the finish without his father. 'A double clear. There won't be many of those.'

Kiri felt a swell of pride at the unexpected praise.

'Walk Foxy around until he cools down,' said Jen. She helped Kiri wash the sweat off, put on a rug and give him some well-earned hay. Listening to the sound of contented munching, Kiri thought she'd never been so happy in her life.

'He was wonderful. He's the best horse in the world.'

'He's got a lot of talent. And I think you're going to do better than you expected.'

Jen went off to ride her own cross-country course, leaving Kiri to gaze dreamily into Foxy's eyes. Her visions of riding the course, over and over again, were interrupted by Marianne Jackson, who'd come to the horsebox park to seek her out.

'You rode the ski jump very well. The best I've seen all day.'

Kiri blushed with pleasure. It was thrilling to get a compliment from someone who was almost a stranger.

Jen came back equally happy. 'Tanker's such fun to ride cross-country. If I can ever make him do a good dressage test, I'll be laughing.'

Now that Foxy had Tanker for company, Jen was able to persuade Kiri to return to the results board. Nearly all the marks in the Under Eighteen class were up and it was obvious that a difficult cross-country course had turned the earlier results inside out.

'You're in the top three!' said Jen, squeezing her arm.

Kiri was overwhelmed. To be in the running for a prize was too much to take in. The last scores went up on the board, one by one, and Jen gasped. 'You came second. Fantastic!'

'Bad luck not being first,' said William, but Kiri didn't care. All that mattered to her was the amazing bond she had felt between her and Foxy as they flew round the cross-country.

'Quick,' said Jen. 'You've got to get into your dressage clothes for the prize-giving in front of Downlands Manor.' Kiri ran to the box, did a fast change and was back in time to hear her name called out by the sponsor along with seven other placed riders. Prizes were handed out, starting with the lowest, until only Kiri and one other remained. Kiri received a blue rosette and an envelope with a tack shop voucher, while the winner got a red rosette and a trophy. As they turned to face the audience, a photographer snapped and Marianne Jackson took the microphone.

'Congratulations to Emma and Kiri. By coming first and second at Downlands, they have qualified for the National Under Eighteen Championship in August. Please give them a big cheer.'

As the applause echoed round them, Kiri felt six feet tall. The no-hoper, the first-timer, the girl who couldn't do a dressage test had qualified for the National Championship.

Foxy nibbled some hay, but he couldn't eat the hard feed – not when the adrenalin was still burning through his veins from galloping and jumping. His muscles twitched and for a moment he was still out there, heart pounding and lungs pumping as he powered up the hill. Again he faced the leap into empty space. A second's hesitation but not from her. 'Go!' her body said and he'd gone. Up into the air. Landed like a cat. On to the next. On and on he'd go with her. For ever.

Chapter 18

Kiri was staring out of the classroom window, jumping round the course at Downlands. She'd done it so many times over the past week that she had every detail of every fence sharp in her mind like a photograph. What she didn't have in her head was the answer Mrs Matheson wanted. That was because she hadn't listened to the question.

'Sorry, can you repeat . . .'

'No I can't.' Mrs Matheson was usually tolerant in her maths class, so it came as a shock to Kiri when she snapped. 'You can take this note to the head right now.'

'Another detention,' thought Kiri, not really caring. She couldn't go to the stables during the week, so what did it matter if she was kept in? She walked as slowly as possible to Miss Carlton's office and, after knocking and entering, handed in the note.

'It's not just Mrs Matheson who's disappointed in

you, Kiri. I've had a lot of complaints about your work, or the lack of it. Detentions don't seem to make any difference, so this time I'll be writing to your father to see if he can find a way of making you pay attention. Now go back to your class and focus.'

Kiri didn't hold it against Mrs Matheson, but she did wish that letter wasn't going to her father. He would never tell her off for doing badly in a subject she found difficult but 'not trying' was a serious crime.

It wasn't until he got home on Friday that he saw the letter.

'Are you unhappy at Denge Academy?'

'No.'

'Then what's the problem?'

'It's boring.'

'What's not boring?'

'Riding Foxy. Playing with Ben. Being at the stables.'

'Carrots and sticks,' said her father. 'That's how you train donkey . . .' He didn't say any more until he was leaving on Sunday, and his pronouncement left Kiri speechless.

'It's so unfair,' she told Roxana later. 'I'll really have to do some work now.'

She explained what her father had decided. If she came first or second in two subjects in the end of term exams, she could go on the four-day South Downs ride organized every year by Aggie. That was the carrot.

If she didn't, the stick came into effect. She'd be banned from going to the stables all through the school holidays.

'That's terrible,' said Roxana. 'Which subjects?'

'He said I could choose.' The girls discussed her options. Maths was the obvious choice because she was good at it, and there wasn't much competition from the rest of the class.

'English?' suggested Roxana.

'Not with that awful woman. She makes it worse than a foreign language.'

'History?'

'Noooo!'

In the end they settled on biology. The teacher, Mr Miles, was easy-going and, as Kiri said, at least it was about animals.

'Will you be able to take Foxy on the South Downs?'

'If only. But Aggie will find me a horse to ride. You can come too.'

'On Mouse?'

'He's too old, poor thing. But you can join in the ride on a bike. That's how I did it before. Dogs can come too and it's great fun. We camp on farms every night.'

Roxana passed her a copy of *Essential Biology*. 'Let's get started.'

Jen looked horrified when she heard about the carrot and stick.

'First or second in two subjects is asking a lot.'

'He knows I came top in maths at my last school.'

'Then you'd better work extra hard. I'm in charge of the South Downs ride this year instead of Aggie, and I'd like your help.'

This was the last weekend that Kiri would be able to ride Foxy. William's doctor had said he could get back in the saddle from the following Saturday and start jumping again in a couple of weeks' time.

Although she'd known it would be hard to give Foxy back, she hadn't been prepared for the agonizing ache in her heart as she rode him out on the marsh for the last time. She told herself she'd be able to see him every weekend and every day in the school holidays, if she did well in the exams. But it wasn't the same. Nothing could match the thrill of riding a horse that loved and trusted her as much as she did him.

The spring sunshine was playing hide and seek with April showers, and the colours of the marsh gleamed in the wet. Red campion hid in emerald grass, and purple speedwell nestled beside the dusty pink of shepherd's cress. These were the flowers that her mother had loved to paint. Kiri realized with a jolt that she hadn't been thinking of her nearly so often since she'd been riding Foxy. She felt guilty for a moment, but she knew her mother would have wanted her to be busy and happy.

As William started riding again and the stables took

up less of her time, school absorbed the rest of it like a sponge. Mrs Matheson pounced on her new interest in maths, swamping her with enthusiasm. Mr Miles lived up to his reputation of being laid-back, but even he couldn't resist a request for extra work.

'What's got into you?' he asked.

Kiri explained the reason and he gave a cynical smile. 'So it's all systems go until July, and in September you'll be back to staring out of the window. Unless I can persuade you to work for work's sake.' He surprised her by lending her a book on the anatomy of the horse and talked about the options open to someone leaving school with good exam results in science. 'You're interested in eventing, which is an expensive sport. But if you became a vet, you could afford to do it.'

Kiri was more inclined to dream of Olympic medals than veterinary college, but occasionally the idea drifted back into her head and she didn't dismiss it completely. She'd love to see her father's face if she announced that she – not Eddie – was going to be the one who got a degree.

Because Kiri and Roxana had similar colouring – dark hair and brown eyes – Tanya and her friends had taunted them, calling them both Gyppos. But now that the two girls were firm friends, they put up a wall of deadly indifference, and the bullies backed off.

'I could report you to Miss Carlton,' Kiri said to

Tanya. 'But why bother? You're just airheads.'

Kiri was still curious to know more about Roxana's family and about Romania. 'What does it look like?'

'Mountains and forests, though we lived in the capital, Bucharest. Our flat was bigger than where we live now, but it was crumbling around us. A leaky roof, damp in winter and lots of power cuts.'

'But it was home,' said Kiri, who couldn't imagine leaving Walland Farm.

'The people living next door despised Roma. They put dog poo through the letter box and once they threw stones at me.'

'No! That's horrible.'

'It was. That's why Mum was so desperate to come to Britain. And my cousins had trouble too.'

A few days later, Kiri suggested they meet up on the following Sunday, but Roxana shook her head.

'Mum likes me to visit Great-grandma.'

'Maybe I could come with you?'

'I don't know . . .' Roxana hesitated for a moment. 'But yes, why not?'

The next Sunday, the girls pedalled over to Lydd. Roxana led the way past the army barracks to a mobile home on the outskirts of the town. The paint was peeling off the walls and the front yard was covered in junk.

'This is it,' said Roxana with an embarrassed smile.

She waved at two boys who were tinkering with an old motorbike.

'Hello, Roxy,' said the eldest cousin. He nodded at Kiri. 'I'm Anton,' he said. 'This is Danut.'

Kiri returned Anton's nod. She saw that he was blushing.

The younger boy, Danut, noticed too. 'Sorry about him,' he said with a grin. 'He is shy. You see, we don't usually get visits from beautiful English girls.'

Kiri, who hated compliments like that, didn't answer.

Danut revved up the bike. 'But you probably think you're too good for us anyway,' he said. 'Everybody else does,' and he gunned the bike out of the yard.

Anton shrugged, as if to apologize, and Kiri smiled back.

'Come and see Great-grandma Cosmina,' he said.

Kiri caught her breath as he took them to a small caravan behind the mobile home. He knocked and pushed open the door.

'Roxana and a foreign friend to see you, Great-grandma.'

Kiri was the foreigner now. She held her chin up and walked into a dark space where all she could hear was the rustle of skirts and the chink of jewellery. She moved forward two paces until she could see dark eyes glittering.

Roxana struck a match to light a candle and Kiri saw an old lady in embroidered skirts and layer after layer of rich shawls. Ropes of gold and turquoise beads hung round her wrinkled neck, and her fingers were encrusted with rings.

She beckoned Kiri closer and spoke in a voice that creaked with age. The words sounded strange and Kiri had no idea if they were Romanian or Roma. Roxana translated.

'Why have you come to see me?'

'Roxana said you can see the future.'

The old lady looked at Kiri carefully but said nothing.

'I have money to pay you,' said Kiri, groping in her pocket. Roxana gasped as she placed sixty pounds on the table next to the old lady – it was all the money she'd saved from Torebridge.

Cosmina gave a small nod.

Kiri straightened her shoulders. 'I want to know what will happen to Foxy and me,' she said. 'Will I get my heart's desire?'

The old lady chuckled. 'Your heart's desire now, or tomorrow or in sixty years' time? Can't imagine yourself old like me, can you?'

There was a long silence broken only by Kiri's quickened breathing and the sound of the old woman muttering under her breath.

'A horse, afraid in the dark. Hunted. Danger.' The words jolted Kiri like an electric shock. Danger for her, or Foxy or both of them? Suddenly Cosmina leant forward and thrust the notes into Kiri's hand. 'Take your money back, child. You're a friend of Roxana and I won't tell you lies. But I won't tell you the truth either.'

Chapter 19

Kiri was awake in the middle of the night, worrying about what Cosmina had seen in the future. When Ben sensed her anxiety, he jumped on to the bed and gave her a lick. A dog was a great comfort, but she wanted someone to talk to.

'Are you asleep?' she asked Roxana, who turned over and groaned.

'Not anymore.'

'Can we go back to your great-grandma and ask her why she wouldn't tell me what she saw?'

'She'll never say.'

'What do you think it was?'

'Heaven knows. Could be anything or nothing at all. Sometimes she doesn'ttell people what she's seen because she thinks it might change the future. She really believes that and she says it's dangerous.'

'I'm worried about Foxy. He could be the one in danger.'

'You can't know that. Go back to sleep.'

Eventually Kiri dozed off but her lack of sleep made Friday classes drag, and she was half asleep when her father got home for the weekend. He burst into the house full of good cheer.

'Steph and I have come to an agreement. We're going to start seeing each other again on the understanding that she never again offers to rescue my business. She's back in England for a few days and she wants to celebrate by taking us all to the races tomorrow. Marina and Roxana too, if they want to come.'

Kiri gave her father a hug. 'That's cool.' She wanted to go to the races, but she still had reservations about Steph.

The next day she got up early to get her work at the stables out of the way and found William already there for an early coaching session with Jen. Aggie had bought some more showjumps and Kiri watched anxiously as he rode round what was now a good-sized course in the paddock. Under Jen's eagle eye, William was riding better and Foxy seemed confident. Kiri was pulled in two directions: glad that Foxy was going so well but miserable because she wasn't riding him.

She hurried home and had just changed into her only smart skirt and the white silk shirt Steph had given her for Christmas, when Steph herself arrived in a flurry of kisses and parcels.

'Presents from America!' she said, giving Jim sparkling wine from California and Kiri the skinniest black jeans she'd ever seen.

'Thank you,' said Kiri, giving Steph a hug, but wondering if the jeans were a bribe.

They all packed into her father's car, an ancient Volvo that had replaced the four by four, and left Ben with Tom for the day. Although Marina was working, Roxana was thrilled to be invited. She'd never been to the races before and they arrived at Lingfield racecourse in high spirits.

'This is my treat to celebrate the end of my court case and my reappearance at Walland Farm,' said Steph, who was looking stunning in an outfit of black and white and a wide brimmed hat. 'There are horses for Kiri and good things to eat and drink for everyone. You've lost weight since I last saw you, Jim.'

When Kiri looked at her father through Steph's eyes, she realized it was true. His cheeks had hollowed, but because she saw him every weekend, she'd failed to notice the gradual change. She slipped her arm through his and gripped it hard. Although they had their ups and downs, the thought of him being ill was frightening.

'What's the matter, Dad?'

'A bit tired and overworked – that's all. Nothing that a day at the races can't cure.'

Steph had bought them tickets to the grandstand and a reserved table in the restaurant with a splendid view of the racecourse.

'Let's eat now,' said Steph, 'and then we can concentrate on the racing.'

'I've never eaten in a place like this.' Roxana was staring at the menu in awe. But as soon as the food arrived, she forgot her inhibitions and wolfed down a seafood starter, fillet steak and strawberry tart, as if that was what she had for lunch every day.

Kiri watched her father chatting and joking with Steph. It still hurt to see him with anyone except her mother, but she could see how Steph cheered him up.

'Are there jumps here like at Downlands?' asked Roxana. Kiri became so busy sorting out her friend's ignorance of all things horsy that she had no more time to worry about her father.

'It's flat racing so no jumps. And today's big race is a trial for the Derby – that's the most lucrative flat race in Britain. The winner is worth millions at stud.' Kiri found them a good place to watch the horses parading before the first race. 'If you want to spot a winner, look for one that's in good condition and not wasting energy by jigging about with excitement.'

'They look spindly compared with Foxy.'

'That's because they're three-year-old thoroughbreds designed exclusively for speed. Foxy's thoroughbred with a bit of Lusitano, which is what makes him just right for eventing.'

Jim and Steph joined the girls at the parade.

'You're too young to bet, but you can advise me where to put my money,' said Steph.

'The grey looks in good shape.' Kiri hoped her knowledge of horses would pay off.

'I like number twelve,' said Roxana. 'He's got a sweet face and a girl jockey.'

Steph went off to place the bets and met them on the grandstand balcony. The moment the horses were out of the starting gates, the racecourse came alive with a hum of anticipation, which rose to a howl of excitement as the horses turned the corner into the final straight. The grey was in the lead until the favourite swept past, but the girl jockey still had a chance. She edged her way forward until Sweetface, as Roxana called him, just had his nose in front. The favourite fought back and they crossed the line in a photo finish. After a tense wait, the announcer gave the race to Sweetface and Kiri clapped Roxana on the back.

'Well chosen!'

'Beginner's luck,' said Roxana, blushing, but everyone could see she was thrilled to have picked the winner.

Kiri was looking forward to the big race because the favourite, Sun Dancer, was trained at a stable on the South Downs. After coming second in the Two Thousand Guineas, he'd become a hot tip for the Derby, and what made him more appealing to Kiri was his colour – a fiery chestnut, like Foxy. So, it came as a big disappointment when the announcement came that he'd been withdrawn. No reason was given and, after a collective sigh of regret, people crowded round the TV screens to find out more.

Stolen. The word went viral through the crowd. Kiri jostled her way closer to the TV.

'Disappeared from his stable overnight . . . reward offered . . . Sussex police mounting a big operation . . . reminiscent of Shergar, the Irish Derby winner stolen by masked gunmen from a stud farm in 1983 and never seen again . . .'

Kiri went cold. Horse thieves were operating in her part of the country. She knew that thieves who went after Derby favourites were unlikely to bother with a small yard like Aggie's, but she couldn't help shivering. Eddie had told her the story of Shergar, and she'd imagined him abandoned and starving before he was shot dead and his body destroyed. Was this the danger which Great-grandma Cosmina had foreseen?

It would be mean to spoil everyone's treat, so Kiri covered up her worries and joined in the fun again. Even without Sun Dancer, the big race had an exciting finish, but the magic had gone out of the day. As they left the racetrack, Steph generously insisted on splitting her winnings between the two girls and Roxana went home in love with racing. Kiri had enjoyed the day too, but she couldn't stop thinking of Sun Dancer and the agony his owner must be going through.

Chapter 20

Kiri was looking forward to half-term, even though she wouldn't be able to ride Foxy. Her father said he'd take time off and spend the whole week at Walland, and he'd hinted that Steph might join them from America. Kiri found she didn't mind the idea of seeing more of Steph, so it came as a double blow when the visit was put off and Jim's business problems dragged him back to the north.

'Never mind,' said Roxana. 'Mum and I can stay all week, and we can have fun with Ben.'

Kiri was glad of her friend's company and when Jen phoned to ask if she wanted to groom for William at a dressage and showjumping competition, she almost said no.

'You go,' said Roxana. 'You'll enjoy looking after Foxy, and I'll be fine here with Ben.'

Kiri was grateful for her friend's generosity. She

cycled over to Torebridge, where Jen was loading Foxy into the horsebox. Kiri checked that the right tack was on board and got in beside Jen.

'What class is William in?'

'The advanced. He wants to see how Foxy measures up against the best event riders – lots of them come here for a practice before a three-day event. But I've advised him to withdraw before the showjumping. The advanced fences will be too high.'

As soon as they arrived, Kiri started getting Foxy ready. After fixing his mane in the Andalusian braid and plaiting his tail, she had plenty of time to put an extra shine on his coat and darken his hooves with oil. She was putting on his saddle and bridle when William arrived with his father. He mounted swiftly and Kiri had to admit that horse and rider looked good together. William was wearing elegant leather boots, a beautifully cut coat and a white stock that set off his tanned face and grey eyes.

The pair of them looked even better in the arena. William had Foxy going so beautifully that he seemed more like an Olympic champion in pure dressage than an eventer. He floated up the centre line and moved round the arena with a combination of power and grace, which would be hard to beat. As he came up the centre for the final salute, Kiri heard a rustle of interest from the spectators.

'Who's that?'

'William Harding. He's a new face in eventing.'

'With a horse like that, he's going places.'

Kiri glowed with pride on Foxy's behalf, and had to admit a reluctant admiration for William.

Kiri's opinion of Foxy's performance was confirmed by an exuberant William, who had just returned from the scoreboard.

'I'm in the lead – miles ahead of everyone else – with only three more to go. And there are some top riders in our class like Zara Phillips and Pippa Funnell. Even my father was impressed, or he will be if I win.' He paused. 'I'm not going to withdraw from the jumping now. Even with a fence down, I'll still win.'

'Are you sure?' Jen looked up with a frown. 'Foxy's been going so well at home. It would be a shame to overface him with advanced fences. He won't have to jump this high when you take him to the next qualifier.' Jen had already told Kiri that William was still hoping to get qualified for the Under Eighteen National Championship.

'I'm going to do it,' he said and marched off to walk the course.

'Can't you stop him?'

'How?' Jen bit her lip. 'It's his father's fault. He's always putting pressure on William to win.'

Kiri put on Foxy's jumping tack with a sinking

heart. Why did William always push things too far? When she saw the course, she sucked in her breath at the size of the fences. She crossed her fingers for luck, and it seemed to be working for the first five jumps. Foxy looked balanced and confident, concentrating on the fences and clearing them effortlessly, even though they were bigger than anything he'd ever jumped before. The trouble came when they turned a corner at the far end of the ring to face a massive wall. Kiri could see the hesitation in Foxy's eyes and she clenched her fists, willing him to keep going, but when William felt the falter in his stride, he panicked. Instead of keeping his hands still and driving forward with his legs, he picked up his stick and gave an almighty whack. Terrified, Foxy bolted into the bottom of the wall and, unable to take off, demolished it completely. William hit him again while he waited angrily for the fence to be rebuilt, and Kiri knew there was no hope of their getting round.

'Please, please retire now,' she thought, 'before Foxy gets hurt.'

She looked at Jen, who was gripping the railing surrounding the ring, but she wasn't allowed to interfere. It had to be the rider's decision. Kiri's hands were shaking as she watched William approach the fence again. Foxy's ears were flat against his head and when William kicked him into a near gallop, the horse's only escape was to duck out at the last moment, sending his rider flying into the wall.

William wasn't hurt, except for his pride, but that was seriously damaged. He remounted, made a tight-lipped bow to the judge and left the arena. He knew better than to beat a horse after elimination – at least in public where he could be reported – but the way his knuckles tightened on the stick told Kiri he wanted to do just that. He dismounted and almost threw the reins at Jen.

'He's dangerous. I'm never going to ride him again.' Jen passed the reins to Kiri and ran after him, but he brushed her off and stormed towards his father in the spectator stand.

Kiri led Foxy back to the box and tried to soothe *his* wounded pride. He stood with his head up and his ears back to show that he was never going to trust another human again, not even her. She took no notice but picked up a sponge and started to wash away the sweat and the fury. She smoothed the welts, which were already appearing where he'd been hit and murmured small words of comfort. Slowly, he lowered his head but still flinched every time she went near his hindquarters.

He was still nervy when they got back to Torebridge, and Kiri was worried.

'Will he ever jump again?' she asked Jen.

'Of course, but only if he trusts his rider.'

'So, what's going to happen to him?'

'I don't know. He could be a wonderful horse for William in pure dressage, but I don't think they'll ever event together. I'll phone the Hardings tomorrow, and see what they decide once William has calmed down.'

The agony of not knowing stretched into the middle of half-term week.

'I've left messages and texted,' said Jen, 'but William's not answering.' Kiri thought she looked anxious too. Her plans for establishing a coaching centre for eventers would suffer if William was bad-mouthing her methods.

'It's so unfair. It wasn't your fault he rode like that.'

'He always rides worse when his father's watching. Grant Harding spends a fortune on his son, but he never lets him forget it.'

Kiri could almost have felt sorry for William if he hadn't been so cruel to Foxy. She compared Grant Harding's treatment of his son with her own father's attitude to his children. He'd been disappointed and angry with Eddie for refusing to go to university, but eventually he'd accepted his son's choice, and now they emailed each other every week.

And what about her? At the time of their bitter quarrel over the sale of Foxy, she'd hated her father, but now she was beginning to see his side of the story.

Perhaps he really hadn't realized how much it would hurt her. She was also beginning to understand the horrendous cost of keeping an eventer. She saw the bills, which went out to the Hardings, and noticed how Jen scrimped to pay for Tanker's keep and entry fees. But the more remote the possibility of owning Foxy, the more determined she became. So when Roxana passed on a message from Jen asking her to come to the stables as soon as possible, she could hardly breathe.

'What's happened?'

'I don't know. Jen said there was good news, and bad.'

What was it with humans? Why didn't they listen? He'd told that man the jump was too high. But he refused to listen, and then he'd lost his temper. Foxy would never forget or forgive that beating. The pain and rage of it swept over him again. His ears flattened and his head snaked forward, ready to threaten anyone who came into his box. Except for her. She knew how to soothe him and drain away the anger. And if she'd been riding him, it would never have happened in the first place. She listened.

Chapter 21

Kiri threw her bike against the fence at Torebridge and ran to find Jen, who was making a cup of tea in her horsebox.

'What is it?'

'Sit down and catch your breath. There's a lot to talk about.'

Kiri wished she would get it over with.

'First the bad news: William wants to sell Foxy.' Jen put a sympathetic arm round Kiri's shoulders as she swallowed a sob. 'But his father wants to get as much money for him as possible. At the moment, all the good eventers have gone home with an image of Foxy as a lovely dressage horse who won't jump. So he wants you to ride him in the Under Eighteen National Championship. If you go clear, he'll be a proven eventer and he'll be worth a lot of money.'

Kiri was torn in two. The thought of riding Foxy

round the championship course was making her heart pound with excitement, but the idea of helping to sell him made her feel like a traitor. And training him all through the summer holidays and riding in the event would make the parting even harder when it happened.

'I can't do it.' The words came out in a wail of pain.

'But by going clear, you would be making sure he goes to a good home where his true worth will be appreciated.'

'Then I *have* to do it.' Kiri ran to Foxy's stable and pressed her face into his neck.

'I'm going to ride you all summer and show everyone that you're the best in the world. And I won't think about what comes next.'

The whole of June passed in a frenzy of working for exams and riding Foxy as often as possible. The lighter evenings meant she could ride after school, but then she had to stay up late to revise. Her father would never withdraw his ultimatum about getting into the top two places in maths and biology. Kiri was afraid of failing to reach her target and getting banned from riding all summer. Roxana was working hard too. She was hoping for a good result in Spanish and praying that she would scrape through in English and maths.

There was also a lot to do before Kiri could be officially entered for the Under Eighteen Championship in Oxfordshire. Her father had to give permission for her to register and compete as a member of British Eventing and the money had to be found for her membership.

'Grant Harding's mean,' said Jen. 'I had to bully him into paying for your membership as well as Foxy's entry fees, and, as William thought, he's refusing to pay you for all the preparation and fitness work.'

The idea of being paid to ride Foxy had never crossed Kiri's mind, so she didn't care. Then a horrible thought kicked her in the gut. 'What about my coaching sessions with you – is he paying for them?'

'They're included in the livery,' said Jen quickly. So quickly that Kiri knew it wasn't true.

'You need the money for Tanker. And I can't afford to pay you.'

Jen looked her straight in the face. 'We both know how much you need the coaching – to improve your flatwork and help restore Foxy's confidence over jumps. I know you can't pay, so you can think of it as an investment.'

'What do you mean?'

'If you go well in the championship, I'll get the credit for coaching you, and that will bring me more clients.'

'No pressure there,' thought Kiri, wondering how she was going to live with herself if she failed the challenge of getting Jen more clients, as well as proving that Foxy was the perfect event horse.

As it turned out, Jen wasn't going to have to rely

on her alone as an advertisement for her coaching skills. Kiri had assumed that William wouldn't be able to buy another horse until after Foxy was sold. But two weeks later he phoned Jen to say he'd persuaded his father to advance him the money.

'You'll have to cut me a deal on the cost of keeping two horses, but if you can do that, I'll have the new one delivered at the weekend.'

When the ramp of the horsebox was lowered, out came a seventeen-hand bay thoroughbred that made Foxy look small. Over the next few days, Kiri discovered that Stanford was an event horse, aged ten, with a good record for getting double clears – no faults in the cross-country or showjumping. She also learned to give his hind legs a wide berth. Stan liked to keep his ears back and his hocks ready to lash out at anyone – horse or human – that came too close. But Jen approved. She said Stan was exactly what William needed to qualify for the championship in a hurry: an experienced jumper with reasonable dressage that could be improved. And he wasn't sensitive like Foxy. He wouldn't take any notice of William's bad temper.

Kiri wished William had stayed away. She was afraid he would sneer at her attempts to get Foxy going well on the flat. And she didn't like his attitude towards Jen. He demanded all of her attention, all of the time, making Kiri feel excluded.

She especially didn't want William to come on the South Downs ride. She was looking forward to riding with Jen and Tanker during the day and having a laugh with Roxana in the evenings. William would just get in the way.

She needn't have worried. As soon as he heard they'd be camping, he ridiculed the whole idea.

'I'm not interested in a pony club jaunt with a load of kids. And besides, Stan will need some work before his event the following weekend. It's his last chance to qualify for the championship.'

Kiri still didn't know what horse Aggie would find her for the trip. Greyling was too old and Maisie was too small. She asked Jen if there was another possibility.

'Why don't you ride Foxy?'

'That would be heaven!' Kiri's heart skipped a beat at the prospect of spending four days and three nights with Foxy on the Downs.

'You'll have to ask William, but I don't see why not.'

It took Kiri a week before she found the courage to put the question. Eventually she picked a moment when Jen had just complimented William on the way he was riding Stan.

'Can I take Foxy on the Downs ride? It would help him get fit.'

'Why can't you take Greyling?'

'Greyling is too old!' Jen was definite. 'Foxy always

performs better when he's had a chance to relax. It will do him good.'

At last, Jen managed to talk William round. Foxy would go on the ride with Kiri, and Stan would stay at Torebridge to be schooled by William. Kiri was longing for the holidays and the ride to start, but between now and then loomed the exams.

It seemed impossibly bad luck that the maths and biology exams were on the same day.

'I can't believe it,' said Roxana. 'It's so unfair.'

'At least it'll all be over quickly.'

It was the eve of Armageddon, as Kiri had decided to call it, and they were revising late into the night at Walland Farm.

'Who is Pythagoras and why should I know about him?' moaned Roxana. 'And what on earth is a "hypotenuse"?'

Kiri dragged herself away from an equation designed to calculate the weekly wage of a plumber and explained Pythagoras's theorem as best she could.

'You're much easier to understand than Mrs Matheson.' Roxana looked guiltily at her watch. 'You've spent a whole hour helping me, instead of getting on with the stuff you need to revise.'

'It doesn't matter. I'm sick of calculating the plumber's wage. I expect we'll get a question about what a banker earns instead. And I know the answer to that.'

'What is it?' Roxana's eyebrows shot up in alarm.

'Millions. Too many of them.' Kiri grinned and pushed the maths books to one side. 'We need some sleep.'

The next morning when Kiri opened the maths paper, she took it as a lucky omen that the first question she saw was on Pythagoras's theorem. She dealt with it confidently and raced through the rest of the questions, as fast as Ben gobbled his dinner. In the afternoon, biology was much harder. A first glance at the paper made her brain freeze, and she sat there for ten minutes not doing anything. She suddenly remembered Foxy refusing to leave the start box. She was doing exactly the same. 'Go!' she told herself and began to write.

'How did you get on?' asked Roxana afterwards.

'Maths was OK but biology . . .'

'I hated them both, except for Pythagoras.'

When all the exams were over, Kiri threw herself into riding. As well as schooling, she and Foxy went for long hacks across the marsh. Cantering along a dyke across a sun-yellowed field, she spotted a hare crouched motionless, hoping it wouldn't be seen by the buzzard hovering above. She felt like a hare herself, but in her case, the buzzard was the biology result.

The news was what she expected: top in maths but third in biology, in spite of all her extra studying and frantic revision.

'Well done in the maths,' said Roxana, who was

delighted to have done well in Spanish and English even though her maths result was dismal. 'And you were nearly second in biology. Perhaps your father will change his mind?'

'He might let me go on working at the stables, but he'll never let me go on the Downs ride.' Kiri was despondent.

By the time her father's car crunched over the gravel at the end of the week, she had his glass ready on the kitchen table and a bottle of his favourite whisky ready to pour.

'Bad news?' he asked after one look at her trembling lips.

'Top in maths but only third in biology.'

He asked more questions about other subjects and percentages before giving her a surprise hug. 'You've worked hard and done brilliantly, but your maths isn't as good as you think.'

'What do you mean?'

'Average 1 and 3 and you get 2.'

'Yes . . .' She couldn't understand what he was getting at.

'So a first and a third average out at second – which was what I asked for. Well done!' He pulled out his wallet and counted five twenty-pound notes, which he pressed into her hand. 'That's for your South Downs ride. You deserve it.'

Chapter 22

It was a perfect morning: bright sunshine but with a nip in the air, which made the horses snort as they were unloaded from boxes and trailers on Bignor Hill, halfway along the South Downs Way. Aggie's ride covered the eastern and western halves of the Way in alternate years, and this summer they were doing the eastern end from Bignor to Eastbourne – a distance of fifty miles. Kiri felt as if she had travelled into another time zone: a place where she could pretend Foxy was hers, and she didn't need to worry about the future.

There were twenty horses and ponies on the ride, as well as cyclists, so the car park was a chaos of riders tacking up, cyclists checking tyres and Aggie's team of volunteers trying to make sure that no one forgot their water bottles or suncream. The volunteers would go ahead every day, taking the luggage, tents and animal feed to farms along the route where Aggie had arranged grazing for the horses and fields for camping.

Kiri waved goodbye to the cyclists who were setting out ahead of the horses. Several of them had brought dogs, and Ben was in a frenzy of excitement running beside Roxana, who'd been persuaded to abandon her boneshaker, in favour of Eddie's geared bike. Before the horse riders mounted, Jen warned them to space themselves out in pairs so the horses didn't think it was a race.

'I'll lead the way and Kiri McFarlane will be at the back. If anyone gets into difficulties, Kiri will help you.'

Kiri was proud of being asked to take the role of backstop but worried in case Foxy had other ideas. He was already prancing around like a two year old. Some of the other riders looked equally anxious and were glad to make use of the mounting block at the edge of the car park. Kiri made Foxy wait until the pair in front of her were well ahead before vaulting into the saddle and setting off.

Bignor Hill was one of the highest points on their route, and the view of rolling farmland made Kiri feel as if she was a skylark, fluttering high above the world.

When, at last, they reached the camping place, they were grateful to the volunteers and cyclists who had put up the tents and got a cooking fire started. After washing down Foxy and turning him out with the other horses, Kiri went to see Roxana, who was thrilled with her day.

'The bike was so easy to ride, and Ben was brilliant. He kept close all day and didn't chase anything. Not even when I almost cycled into a sheep!'

The two of them were sharing a tent. Ben joined them too.

The ride was blessed with fine weather, and Kiri had the feeling that she was living in the calm before a storm. Every morning they woke to clear skies, and Kiri's face and arms gradually tanned to a deep gold. On the last night, they camped at a farm next to the trainer's yard where Sun Dancer had been stolen. The farmer, who joined them round their campfire, couldn't stop talking about it.

'Lovely horse he was, worth millions. I hear the owner's devastated.'

'Did you notice anything suspicious?' asked Jen.

'There was a van parked in the lane the day before but I didn't get its number.'

'What a shame.'

'I heard the driver and another bloke – a young one, I think – as they were walking back from the van. Couldn't hear much of what they said, but the younger one called out the name Mark. He seemed to be protesting about something. I heard him say, "It's not good," and then he repeated a strange word: "varog", but I couldn't tell you what *that* meant. The driver didn't say much, just growled, "Get in the van."'

Roxana got up abruptly and walked away, even though her plate was still full. After a while, Kiri went to look for her and found her leaning on the gate of the field where Foxy and the other horses were grazing. Her eyes were wet and her hands were gripping the fence as though she was going to lift it off its hinges.

'What's the matter?'

Roxana gulped without answering.

'You can't just stand here crying without saying why.'

'I know where those men came from.'

'How?'

'*Varog*. It didn't make sense to the farmer but it makes sense to me. "Vă rog" is Romanian for "please". The younger man was Romanian. He must have been pleading with the English man not to make him do something. The day before Sun Dancer was stolen.'

'You can't be sure they were thieves, they might have been talking about

something completely different.'

'I know someone called Mark. He's not a good man. He offers young Romanian men work. At first they are happy. But it turns out to be bad work – illegal. They don't want to do it, but he threatens them. If I tell the police, innocent Romanians may get in trouble.'

Kiri put her arm round Roxana. 'You haven't got

any evidence. The farmer didn't see the men doing anything wrong. And he may have misheard. The police will laugh at you if you tell them what you've just told me.'

Roxana wiped her face with her sleeve. 'I don't want to go to the police. But think how I'd feel if Foxy or another horse got stolen, and I hadn't done anything to stop them.'

'It won't happen. Whoever's got Sun Dancer will be too scared to draw attention to themselves with another theft.'

The girls went back to their tent. After a while Kiri heard Roxana's breathing change to the rhythm of sleep, but she stayed awake for a long time. She couldn't get the image of Sun Dancer and his grieving owner out of her head.

Chapter 23

As soon as they got back from the South Downs ride, Jen called William and Kiri to what she called a 'council of war'.

'You did brilliantly in your qualifiers, but the championship will be a much greater challenge. I want to see both of you with rosettes, but it's going to take a lot of hard work.'

She explained that the championship was a three-day event: dressage on day one, cross-country on day two and showjumping on the final day.

'Don't worry,' she said. 'I'll give you all the help I can, and it's not long till the residential training course for everyone who's qualified in the region.'

Jen told William and Kiri that they needed to be fit, as well as their horses. 'We'll run on the beach – it'll be fun.'

The next day they set out three abreast along

Camber Sands with Ben dashing ahead of them. Jen's eyes danced with mischief as she challenged them to keep up with her. Kiri saw William's jaw clench with determination. She knew he'd hate to be beaten by a girl. He flew past Kiri, but she knew how to pace herself and when Jen and William finally stopped, she wasn't far behind. William collapsed on to the sand with his lungs heaving while Kiri and Jen were quick to recover. They sat and watched Ben chasing a windsurfer.

'I love this part of the world,' said Jen. 'Look how the sea changes colour as it gets deeper.'

'Ice cream?' offered William. 'We need something cold after all that running.'

'William's not all bad,' said Jen, watching him walk to the cafe. 'You have to remember the stress he's under.'

Kiri shook her head. 'He shouldn't have hit Foxy like that.'

'No, he shouldn't.' Jen sighed. 'But I wouldn't want a father like his.'

On the eve of the residential course, Jen drove the two horses and Kiri to the training centre where Marianne Jackson was waiting to greet them.

'You're the first to arrive so choose whichever stables you like.'

Kiri put the horses in adjoining loose boxes and

went to fetch her tack. She was so nervous that she tripped over her reins outside the stable door.

'Relax,' said Jen. 'You'll have a great time.'

Kiri felt lonely as Jen waved goodbye. Some of the other team members were unloading their horses and bringing them over to the stables, chatting loudly to one another, but she was too shy to join in. She felt like an imposter among these confident, rich young people.

William arrived with his usual squeal of brakes and was only just in time for the team meeting. Mrs Jackson welcomed them and talked about team ethics.

'Riders compete both as individuals and team members. You'll be competing as an individual *against* the other members of your team but *with* them against the seven other regions. The team is paramount, so I want to see everyone giving each other plenty of support and encouragement.'

Kiri realized she was holding her breath. She felt under enormous pressure. As well as worrying about the team, she had to protect Jen's reputation and ensure Foxy's future.

Although most of the riders were staying at the centre, William and an older girl called Sarah had decided to go home each night.

'Do you want a lift?' asked William.

'Cool. But I've got to sort my horse out first.'

'Kiri's staying here to look after my two. I'm sure

she'll be happy to do yours as well.'

Kiri bristled but said nothing. She didn't see why she should do Sarah's horse, but if this was what being part of a team meant, she had to agree.

'That's taking the mickey!' The speaker was a boy with floppy brown hair and very blue eyes. His horse, a bay called Bramble with a white blaze, was stabled next to Foxy. 'I'll give you a hand if you like. I'm Sam Paxman, by the way.'

'Thanks.' Kiri smiled shyly at him. Maybe she would make some friends here after all.

After settling the horses down for the night, Sam and Kiri walked over to the equestrian centre for a meal with the rest of the team. Most of them were seventeen or eighteen and were allowed to sleep in their horseboxes. Only Kiri and a fifteen-year-old girl, called Viv, had been given a room inside the centre.

Viv had long red hair and freckles and always seemed to be laughing. 'You know Sam's got the five-star suite?' she asked Kiri, winking at Sam across the table.

When Kiri looked baffled, Sam explained with a grin that he was going to spend the night sleeping on the metal floor of his trailer.

'Will you be all right?' Kiri asked him.

'I'm used to roughing it.' Sam shrugged. 'We've never had the money for a horsebox with a living area.'

So they weren't all rich kids except her! Kiri felt a

wave of relief, then said in a rush, 'My box belongs to my coach. It's not very smart, but there's a bed over the cab and I'm sure she wouldn't mind you using it.'

Sam smiled. 'Sounds good to me. Thanks, Kiri. I'll take up your offer if it gets too uncomfortable in the trailer.'

The next day started with all eight horses performing the championship dressage test. Kiri was last to go. She didn't make any mistakes, but she let Foxy slouch round the arena like a donkey.

'Accurately ridden,' was Mrs Jackson's comment. 'But Foxfire has wonderful paces and you could get a lot more out of him.'

'I'll show you,' offered William.

Kiri's face was burning. William made it sound as if he was doing the team thing by offering to help, but she felt humiliated. As usual, Foxy seemed taller, stronger and more powerful in William's hands.

Kiri was close to tears of frustration. After being ridden by William, Foxy did go much better, and she could feel the power underneath her. If only she could create it herself.

Early the following morning, Kiri mucked out and fed all three horses and was having breakfast with Sam and Viv when William hurried into the dining room.

'The horses aren't groomed yet.'

'We don't start until ten, so there's plenty of time,'

said Kiri, who'd just spread marmalade on her second piece of toast.

'No there isn't! A journalist is coming to write a piece about me and his photographer will be here in a quarter of an hour.'

Sam raised his eyebrows, and Kiri guessed he thought she was an idiot for jumping to obey William's every whim. But it was different for him. Even if he was short of money, he had his own horse and could do what he liked. She stuffed the toast in her mouth and followed William out to the stables.

'Can you do a quick braid? Stan can have a loose mane but I want to emphasize that Foxfire's part Lusitano breeding.'

Kiri worked fast and had Foxy braided and brushed by the time William had dusted the straw off Stan's back. She ran to the tack room and gave William's two best head collars a wipe over, so that the leather glowed and the brass buckles shone.

'Here they are.' William pointed at the van pulling into the parking area. Kiri held the horses while he went and chatted to the journalist.

'Can you move them on to the grass with the house in the background?' asked the photographer, who introduced himself to Kiri as Jack Dixon.

'What a beautiful horse!' he said, looking at Foxy's flaming chestnut coat. 'There. Stand with your head close to his.' He snapped away until Kiri forgot to be self-conscious.

William bustled over and took the reins of both horses. 'Like this,' he told the photographer, standing between Foxy and Stan and giving the lopsided smile which Kiri had noticed he always used to charm strangers. Jack's stare told Kiri he didn't take kindly to being bossed about, but he didn't say anything. He just took three or four pictures then started putting his gear away.

'Are you riding both horses in the championship?' asked the journalist.

'The rules don't allow that,' said William quickly. 'So one of them has to be ridden by my stable girl.' Without giving Kiri's name or introducing her, he walked back to the van with the journalist.

Jack smiled at Kiri. 'He's not going to let your picture get in the paper. Give me your name and address and I'll send you a print. You'll like it, I promise.'

On the last day of training over cross-country fences, Kiri felt she had a lot to prove. When they came to the water jump, Mrs Jackson told Kiri, William and Sam they could take whatever route they chose. Kiri trusted herself and Foxy to jump the advanced fence and was longing to show everyone that their cross-country would make up for their earlier mistakes.

'I'll go first,' she offered, turning Foxy's pricked ears towards the jump.

'No!' William said immediately. 'I won't have you risking my horse over the difficult route. The way you've been riding the past two days, I don't trust you to jump anything.'

'William!' Mrs Jackson's voice cracked like a whip, but Kiri's self-control finally snapped.

'You pig!' she yelled at William. 'You've been trying to show me up all the time we've been here, and now you want to stop me doing the one thing I'm good at.'

'You're no good at any of it,' he bit back.

'Enough!' Mrs Jackson strode between them. 'You'll both go straight to the stables without jumping another fence. And I want to see the two of you in my office as soon as I get back.'

Kiri walked Foxy back to the centre as far away from William as possible. Mutinous tears poured down her face. The thought of apologizing to William was impossible, but she knew that was what Mrs Jackson would expect. And she minded dreadfully not jumping the water complex. She'd been looking forward to it all day.

As soon as she'd settled Foxy and wiped the tears off her face, she went to the office and found William already there. They waited in hostile silence.

'You've both behaved disgracefully and you owe me, and each other, an apology. Judging by today's display you're unfit to be on any team.' Mrs Jackson sat down at her desk and glared at both of them.

'Sorry, William.' Kiri got the words out even though they threatened to stick in her throat. She turned to Mrs Jackson and found it easier to make a genuine apology to her. 'Sorry I lost it. It won't happen again.'

William said nothing until the silence stretched out unbearably. 'Sorry to upset you, Marianne,' he barked abruptly, and got up to leave.

'I'm Mrs Jackson to you, and you haven't yet apologized to Kiri.'

'Sorry.' He spat the word out as he walked through the door.

'Wait,' said Mrs Jackson as Kiri got shakily to her feet to follow him outside. 'If it's any consolation, I think you rode very well today, and you were provoked. But you have to learn to maintain your self-control under all circumstances.'

'I shouldn't have said anything,' said Kiri miserably. 'But I so wanted to jump that fence.'

'I think you would have cleared it safely; otherwise I wouldn't have given you the choice. But riding someone else's horse can be difficult. They do have the final say. Now cheer up and catch up with the rest of the team. I'm sure they'll want to congratulate you for the way you went today.'

When Kiri joined the others, Viv gave her a hug.

'What a total brat!' she said. 'I'd have pushed him

into the muck heap.'

'He's gone with Sarah and good riddance too,' said Sam. 'If ever you need help dealing with William – or anyone else – just give me a call. I'll sort them out for you.'

'Ooh, listen to the tough guy!' Viv's face was creased up with amusement.

Kiri laughed too, but it felt good to have people on her side.

They gathered in the dining room for a last cup of tea and cake, and then they were loading up and leaving.

'How was it?' asked Jen, who'd come to drive Kiri and the horses home.

'Mrs Jackson said I rode the cross-country well,' said Kiri, 'but there were some awful moments too.'

'Always are in eventing. But I bet you made some new friends.'

'I did.' Kiri smiled as she thought of Viv's loud laugh and Sam's offer of help. 'Really good ones.'

When the *Rye Observer* was published a week later, Roxana was outraged. She came out of Aggie's bungalow waving the paper.

'There's a lovely photo of Foxy but nothing about you!'

Kiri looked at the picture of William standing between Stan and Foxy and smiled. Jack had got his revenge. He'd managed to catch William at a moment when the charming smile looked more like a leer.

Kiri had already received her prints in the post and Jack was right: they were beautiful. Her favourite was propped up on her dressing table and she felt a warm glow whenever she looked at it.

'He calls you his stable girl,' said Roxana, reading the article over her shoulder.

'Well, that's what I am,' said Kiri sadly. 'I wish I was Foxy's owner but I'm not.'

The worst thing about the article came at the end when William told the journalist he thought Foxy would be worth £12,000 if he did well in the championship. Kiri felt it like a kick in the gut.

'That much?' said Roxana, aghast. 'It's the price of a new car. Two new cars.'

'I know. That's why I'll never be able to buy him.'

Roxana was leaving with Aggie to help her do some shopping in Rye and Jen had taken two days off to visit her sister, so Kiri was alone at Torebridge apart from one of the clients, who kept an eye on the stables when Jen was away. Foxy was having a day off, enjoying the meadow grass at the far end of the farm, and Kiri had offered to help Jen by exercising Tanker. As she led him through the gate, she saw a man walking towards her. He was short and broad with a peaked cap pulled down low so that it shaded his eyes.

'Can I help you?' she asked. It was rare for anyone to walk this way unless they were coming to the stables.

'I'm looking for my dog – a black Lab. He ran off chasing a rabbit and hasn't come back.'

'Dogs! I hope you find him soon.' Kiri knew just how he felt. She was always worrying about Ben running off. 'I'm riding across the marsh, so I'll keep a lookout for him.'

The man nodded in thanks and slipped past, looking about him as though considering where to search next.

It was a day when the harsh light of high summer picked out every detail of the landscape. She could see for miles across the flat grassland, but the flocks of white sheep grazed peacefully without any sign of being disturbed by a rabbit-hunting dog. And when she listened for the sound of barking, all she could hear was the buzz of insects and the scrape of Tanker's hooves on the path.

The smell was wrong. Foxy flared his nostrils as the man approached with a carrot in his outstretched hand. The carrot smelled good, with an irresistible aroma of sweet starch pulled fresh from the earth. But it was overlaid by a sour tang of fear. Foxy's muscles bunched, ready for flight, and he swivelled his ears to listen for whatever was making the human afraid. Nothing. Nothing except the familiar sound of horses' teeth tearing at dry grass and the swish of tails brushing away flies. Foxy's eyes followed the man's every move, but it was a smooth approach with a soft tread and a steady hand. Nothing to be afraid of. The smell of carrot grew stronger until Foxy could almost taste the nutty crunch of it. He stretched out his powerful neck but before his teeth closed on the treat, a thin wire was flicked over his nose and twisted until spears of pain lanced into his brain. The man tightened the noose by winding it round a stick and the agony became unbearable.

Chapter 24

Tanker was enjoying the outing so much that Kiri was tempted to go all the way to the sea. During the summer, horses weren't allowed on Camber Sands in the middle of the day but, even if she couldn't splash through the water, she wanted to smell the salt in the air and watch the kite surfers skimming the waves.

'Better not,' she thought. She still had a lot of work to do at Torebridge.

So, instead of continuing along the road to Camber, she swung round in a loop, which would bring her back to the stables on a seldom-used bridle path. About halfway along, Tanker started neighing loudly and, as they turned a bend in the path, the nightmare began. With her brain in slow motion, Kiri recognized a familiar chestnut head coming towards her. It was Foxy, being ridden bareback by someone. His cap was pulled down low, shading his eyes – it was the man who'd said he was looking for his dog.

'Foxy!' she screamed as her brain caught up with her eyes. But the thief's reactions were quicker. He yanked Foxy to the left, kicked him down the dyke into a field of potato plants and started galloping. Kiri, her mind now sharp with anguish, urged Tanker after them. By the end of the field Tanker was closing the gap but she had no idea what to do next. Then she saw a line of reeds ahead of them. They marked the boundary of the next farm and were the answer to her prayer – if she had the guts to do what she was thinking.

She kicked Tanker on until he was galloping just behind Foxy. The thief glanced over his shoulder. Judging her distance, she made Tanker surge past Foxy towards the reeds. 'Now!' She kicked again hard and felt him fly into the air when he saw the expanse of water beyond the reeds. They hung in the air for what felt like minutes and then his hooves thudded safely on to the far bank. Another thud and Foxy was racing past her, riderless.

She'd done it! She'd trusted Tanker to jump the ditch and Foxy to follow him, hoping the unexpected leap would throw the bareback thief off. She looked behind but there was no sign of him: she hoped he'd fallen in the water. It was another mile before Foxy slowed to a trot and she managed to grab his reins. Her heart was pounding. She wanted to call for help on her mobile, but she needed both hands to hold the reins of the two horses.

She brought them both to a walk and headed for a lane which would bring them back to the stables without going anywhere near the ditch. Kiri was still shaking when they got to Torebridge, but the horses clattered into the yard looking as if they'd done nothing more than complete a cross-country course, which, in a way, they had.

She washed them down and it wasn't until she sponged Foxy's head that she noticed the cruel mark around his nostril. 'He twitched you,' she muttered angrily. Twitching had once been used by vets because it was the only safe way to operate on a horse, but now the practice had been replaced by modern sedatives. Kiri examined every inch of Foxy, but could find nothing else wrong. She buried her face in his mane and cried with relief. She'd come so close to losing him.

As soon as her breathing was back to normal, she reached for her mobile. She knew she should call the police but something held her back. She dialled Jen's number several times without success. Roxana and Aggie were back with their shopping but the first thing Aggie would do, if told about the attempted theft, was call the police. Kiri didn't want them involved. She waited until she could attract Roxana's attention.

'Something terrible has happened. I've got to talk to you.'

They went to Jen's horsebox where Kiri made cups

of hot chocolate with hands that were still shaking.

'Kiri, what's wrong?'

'A man tried to steal Foxy. I stopped him, but I'm frightened he'll try again.' She described the chase. 'I couldn't face going back to look on my own, so I don't know if he ran away or if he's lying there unconscious.'

'Why haven't you called the police?'

The two girls looked at each other, neither daring to say what they were both thinking. In the end it was Kiri who found the courage to say it.

'I was afraid it might cause trouble for you.' She described the man's stocky build and his distinctive, low cap.

Roxana went pale under her tan. She got out her phone and scrolled through her photos. 'Look.'

Kiri stared at a photo of Roxana at a party with her cousins, Anton and Danut. Standing behind them, with his hands firmly on the boys' shoulders, was the man who'd tried to steal Foxy. He was smiling as though he'd just won the lottery. Kiri looked into her friend's eyes, appalled. Was she going to have to choose between protecting Foxy and destroying Roxana's family?

'That's him,' she whispered. 'Who is he?'

'Mark,' Roxana confirmed with a shudder. 'At first he was kind to my cousins, telling them he would help them make a life for themselves in England. He gave them work, good work – just loading things on to lorries – but then things changed. He wanted them to steal. They refused but he threatens them. When my mother saw this photo, she told me never to have anything to do with him.'

'I'm not going to tell the police if it'll put you in danger. Will it?'

Roxana was crying. 'If Mark thinks I've identified him, he could take revenge on my family as well as me. You don't know what these people are like.'

'But you do, and you're frightened, so I'm not going to the police. I'm going to deal with this myself.'

Chapter 25

There was one thing that Kiri knew had to be done at once. She had to return to the ditch and find out if Mark was lying there injured or even dead.

'I can't come with you, ' said Roxana, 'he might recognize me, but you can't go alone either!' Her sobs got louder.

'Don't worry. I've summoned reinforcements,' said Kiri with a grin. 'And you've got to stop crying. None of this is your fault.'

Kiri's first thought had been to enlist Jen, but she wasn't answering her phone and, even if she did, she'd probably insist on the police being called. Then Kiri came up with a brilliant idea. Sam Paxman. He'd told her she could call on him for help anytime and, although he might not have had the pursuit of a dangerous criminal in mind, she thought he'd be up for it. She was right. After a surprised pause, and a few direct questions, he promised to be there as soon as he could.

'This is my brother, Rob,' said Sam as he got out of a battered Land Rover an hour later. 'He's a builder.' Rob looked like Sam, only two sizes larger – a comforting sort of person to have on a mission like theirs. When Kiri explained that a visit to the ditch was the first thing on her list, Sam got a first aid kit out of the back of the car, while Rob picked up a crowbar.

As they approached the ditch, there was no sign of a body. They moved cautiously up to the edge of the reeds and peered over them into the water. Nothing there either, and no sign that anyone had dragged themselves out of the ditch and through the reeds to dry land. He must have got away unscathed.

'Why did the thief choose Foxy?' asked Sam.

'I expect it was the article in the local paper,' said Kiri. 'It said he was worth thousands of pounds.'

'He'll have had a plan to get Foxy away,' said Sam. 'There must have been a horsebox or trailer waiting nearby.'

'Of course!' Kiri suddenly remembered a grey horsebox that had been parked on the lane near the entry to the bridle path. She wished she'd taken its number. But they had other ways of tracking the thief down.

As soon as they got back, Kiri made an excuse to talk to Roxana away from the boys. 'You've got to phone Anton and find out where Mark lives.'

'He might not tell me if he knows my reason for asking. He's very protective – doesn't want me to get involved.'

Roxana thought for a moment before dialling. She talked in Romanian for a few minutes and then smiled triumphantly. 'I told Anton I was going to be knocking on doors in Lydd to raise money for a charity and wanted to *avoid* Mark's house. He doesn't know the exact address, but he thinks it's in Dengemarsh Road, between the army camp and the sea.'

Kiri told Sam and Rob she'd had a tip-off about the identity of the thief. She said she couldn't reveal her source but she wanted to go and look at the man's place and see if there was anywhere a horse could be hidden.

'Why don't you go the police?' asked Rob.

Kiri looked him straight in the eyes. 'I don't want to call the police until I'm sure. If I'm wrong about this man, it could get a friend of mine into trouble.'

'Fair enough,' said Rob. 'We'll go take a look.'

Kiri insisted on leaving Roxana behind with Aggie.

'There'll be lots of horse owners here this evening, so you won't be alone, and we can't risk Mark seeing you and knowing you're involved.'

Roxana agreed reluctantly but insisted that Kiri take Ben with her for extra protection. They drove to Lydd in silence except for some whining from Ben, who sensed the tension inside the Land Rover. From the centre of the town, they drove past the camp on to Dengemarsh Road, which went through a dilapidated business park. There were some run-down repair shops, metal scrap yards and a builders merchant.

'Stop a moment,' said Rob. He went into the builders merchant and came out a few minutes later, looking pleased with himself. 'I told them I was hoping to get a big building contract nearby. Then asked if they'd seen any horseboxes being driven along this road. The answer was "yes". They think it came from somewhere in the direction of the nuclear station at Dungeness.'

Sam drove on until the road became a rough stone track squeezed between army land and the deserted gravel dunes of a nature reserve.

'Look!' said Kiri, her heart suddenly tight in her chest. 'A horsebox, and it's grey.'

'Don't stop,' said Rob urgently. 'We don't want them to suspect anything.'

'I know this road,' said Kiri. 'It's a dead end, but there's a place to park when we get to the sea.'

They pulled up under an army watchtower on the shore, but no soldiers were on watch and there were no other cars. It was an isolated place. Wire fences prevented access to the power station and the army firing range. And although the shingle beach stretched all the way from Dungeness to Camber Sands, it was blocked by the firing range in the middle. Kiri looked at the tide lapping the pebbles, which burned red in the setting sun. She'd been here before with her mother, but it felt like a million years ago.

'Take this,' said Sam, getting a bridle out of the Rover and giving it to Kiri. 'If we're going to rescue a racehorse, it might come in handy.' Rob had his crowbar and some rope while Sam put an iron horseshoe in his jacket pocket – whether for luck or a weapon, Kiri couldn't tell. They walked back the way they'd come with Ben trotting at Kiri's side. Threatening notices appeared all the way along the army range saying 'Danger, Ministry of Defence'. And there was menace in the humming that came from the high voltage wires on the electricity pylons.

'I don't like those things,' said Sam. 'Someone once dared me to climb one but I wouldn't do it. Too easy to get yourself fried.' Kiri shuddered and he reached out to take her hand. 'Don't worry, no one's going to get hurt.'

When they reached the farm where the horsebox was parked, there was no one about. They hid behind an old shed on the opposite side of the road and waited. Kiri could hear a growl simmering at the back of Ben's throat, and she put her hand on his collar to warn him to be quiet. After three-quarters of an hour, the door of the farmhouse opened and a fair-haired man walked out. He was smaller than Mark, and Kiri wondered if she'd got it all wrong. He disappeared into one of the outbuildings and came out again with a bucket and a net full of hay.

'There must be a horse here,' whispered Kiri.

'Wait,' said Sam. 'We need to see more.'

The fair-haired man went back to the farmhouse and banged on the door. 'I'm not going into the barn alone.'

Another man came to the door. At first he was in silhouette, but when he stepped into the pool of light from a lamp over the door, she knew.

'That's Mark,' she said, clutching hold of Sam.

The smile Mark had worn on the footpath had been replaced by a scowl.

'Give me the bucket, if you're such a coward.' He unlocked a padlock on the door of a large steel barn and took the feed and hay inside.

'The animal's eating now. It won't bother you while you bring some water and clean up the mess inside.' Mark went back into the farmhouse with a contemptuous shake of his head.

'Now's our chance,' said Kiri. 'It's got to be Sun Dancer in there.'

'Rob and I will deal with the guy,' said Sam, 'while you get the horse outside.'

'There may be more men in the house with Mark,' said Rob. 'If they hear us and come out, Sam and I will lure them up the road towards Lydd. You get away as far and as fast as you can.'

Chapter 26

Kiri's legs were trembling as they crossed the yard, clinging to the shadows until they reached the barn door. Kiri pushed Ben flat to the ground and hissed 'Stay!' while Sam slowly opened the door.

The fair-haired man was shovelling dirty straw into a wheelbarrow. He had his back to the door and his whole attention was fixed on a big horse, which had its ears back and its hindquarters swinging in his direction. Kiri's heart leapt when she saw the chestnut coat and two white socks – Sun Dancer!

Sam moved catlike across the barn floor and clamped a hand over the man's mouth while Rob tied his hands behind his back and gagged him with a rag.

Kiri moved softly over to the horse and patted him, taking no notice of his rolling eyes. 'You'll be safe with us,' she whispered and went on stroking his neck until some of the tension leached out of his muscles. She couldn't rush this moment, even though every muscle in *her* body was screaming 'Go'. She rubbed the horse's nose and, to her huge relief, he lowered his head enough for her to slip the bit into his mouth and pull the bridle over his ears.

She gave a thumbs-up sign to the boys and led the horse to the door. Now came the difficult part. She had to get Sun Dancer across the yard and into the road without alerting Mark. For a moment the horse stood still with his nostrils quivering, taking in the strange smells. He must have been locked up in the barn for months. She patted him again and urged him forward. The clop of his hooves on the hard ground sounded loud enough to wake the dead, but there were raised voices inside the farmhouse and Kiri prayed they were too busy arguing to notice. A minute later they were out of the yard and Sun Dancer was walking up the track with the white tip on Ben's tail moving ahead of them like a beacon in the dark.

The sound she was dreading, a yell of fury, came when they were about a hundred metres away. Without thinking, she vaulted on to Sun Dancer's back and nearly fell off when he jinxed sideways in surprise. Clinging on with all her strength, she heard Mark shouting orders.

'You go after the boys in my van. I'll deal with the horse and silence the girl.'

Kiri froze with terror. The guy in the barn must

have given a description, and now Mark would have guessed who she was. The only way he could get rid of the evidence and the witness against him would be to kill her and Sun Dancer.

Her hands were trembling so much that she could hardly hold the reins, but she had to try and get to safety. She kicked Sun Dancer into a trot, dreading the sound of pursuit and praying that his delicate legs would cope with pounding down a stony track in the dark. Luckily for her it wasn't pitch black. Lights from the power station cast an eerie glow, and she peered into the gloom for a way into the nature reserve. The wire fence stretched ahead unbroken and although she might have tried to jump it on Foxy, it was asking too much of a three-year-old thoroughbred.

Expecting to hear the sound of a vehicle coming down the track behind them, she searched desperately for somewhere to hide. When she reached the army watchtower by the sea, there was nowhere else to go. She reined Sun Dancer to a halt and listened. Nothing except the slap and suck of waves on pebbles. Had Mark given up? Ben would bark if he approached on foot, but she wasn't going to wait there, trapped, until he did.

There was heavy security fencing barring access to the power station, but the fence enclosing the firing range didn't go right down to the sea. The only thing to keep people out was another notice saying 'Danger,

Ministry of Defence'. Could she ride along the edge of the firing range to Camber Sands? It might be physically possible but every fibre of her being screamed no. Because Denge Academy was on the outskirts of Lydd and not far from the army camp, the students were given endless lectures on the dangers of trespassing on the range. It was in use most days of the year. Even if it wasn't active now, there was a chance of getting killed by treading on an unexploded shell lying just below the surface of the dunes. They'd had a school visit by a sergeant who seemed to enjoy describing what modern explosives could do to the human body.

She was still hesitating when her mind was made up by the crack of a high velocity rifle. Sun Dancer shied and the hackles on Ben's back went up. Was it the army? Another shot was fired, and Kiri heard the ping of a ricochet off the watchtower. She went ice cold. This was no soldier. This was Mark trying to kill her.

For a moment she was disoriented, not knowing where the shots were coming from, but then there was a flash in the blackness high above and she guessed. Mark had climbed up an electricity pylon so he could pick her off at his leisure. Sobbing with the terror of a trapped animal, she kicked Sun Dancer down the shingle to the edge of the sea and crouched low over his neck. It was hopeless, but she had to try and get away. Another shot echoed from the pylon, and she heard the zip of the bullet into the pebbles. There was no escape. She was going to die.

A bang. A jagged flash ripped open the night sky, burning long, bright and deadly, followed by the smell of burning flesh drifting on the wind. Kiri couldn't look. Wouldn't. Couldn't bear to imagine the body hanging from the wires.

Mark was dead, killed by the hundreds of thousands of volts humming through the wires. Her lungs were heaving and she wanted to turn back. But she wasn't going anywhere near the thing still burning on the pylon. And what if a friend of Mark's was waiting for her, lusting for revenge? She had to go on.

The terror on the beach had left her in deep shock, but she tried to calm her breathing and steady her hands for the sake of Sun Dancer. Horses were quick to pick up emotions from their riders and the last thing she needed now was to be riding a bolting thoroughbred across a firing range.

She whispered encouraging words and persuaded him to start the long trek along the beach to Camber. He was nervous of the pebbles shifting under his hooves, so she tried to pick a route across plants, which grew just above the tideline. It was a long ride – nearly five miles – and she was grateful for the comforting presence of Ben, who trotted patiently behind Sun Dancer. After a while the moon rose, lighting her path and bathing the firing range in shimmering light. A silvered tank buried in a dune, an empty watchtower and a railway track leading nowhere gave the journey a dream-like quality. Kiri needed the space to distance herself from the horror she'd witnessed.

A lifetime later she reached the firm sands of Camber. She thought of calling the police. Then couldn't face it. She needed Sam or Roxana, but when she pulled out her mobile the battery was flat. All she wanted now was to get home. She would put Sun Dancer in Foxy's stall in the barn and fall into the oblivion of sleep.

Things turned out differently. When she arrived at the gate to Walland Farm, the house was ablaze with lights. Willing hands helped her slide to the ground and Sam took the reins.

'I was worried sick about you!'

'I worried about you and Rob too. But I hoped you'd get away.'

'Go inside the house. I'll look after Sun Dancer until his trainer gets here. He's on his way.'

A tear-stained Roxana and an anxious Marina hurried her indoors.

'I called your father and he'll be here in the morning,' said Marina. 'But now bed and no one – not even the police – will be allowed to disturb you.'

When Kiri woke up, her father was at her bedside. Pale

and drawn from the long drive through the night, he held her in his arms and spoke in a voice grating with strain.

'Promise me you'll never give me a fright like that again.'

'I'm sorry . . .'

'Don't be sorry. You were wonderfully brave, but I never want to go through another night thinking . . .' He couldn't finish the sentence.

She had to tell her story over and over again. First to her father, then to Roxana and, in mind-numbing detail, to the police.

'Why didn't you call us immediately after the attempt to steal the horse?' asked the policewoman.

'I didn't think you'd believe me.' Kiri was determined to keep the link between Mark and Roxana secret.

'What made you and the Paxman brothers look in the area of Dengemarsh Road?'

'I go to school near Lydd, and I sort of remembered seeing a grey horsebox driving that way. Like the one parked at the end of the bridleway.' Kiri opened her eyes wide and looked directly at the policewoman. It was her first big lie, but she was sure Sam and Rob would back her up if needed. The interview went on until her father, who by law had to be present, put a stop to it.

'Enough. My daughter's had a shattering twenty-four hours – most of it doing your job for you. She's tracked down a gang of horse thieves, rescued a valuable racehorse, been shot at with a high-powered rifle and witnessed a horrendous death. She needs time to get over it.'

The next few days were quiet. The news of Sun Dancer's recovery was released to the press, but not the details of how he was rescued. The police had asked the McFarlanes to keep quiet about Kiri's role in the affair while they continued to interrogate Mark's associates. Kiri and her father were only too glad to go along with the request. The last thing they wanted was to be mobbed by the media. Roxana had told Aggie and Jen what happened but not about Mark. They too were sworn to secrecy.

To Kiri's disappointment, Sun Dancer had been collected by his trainer while she was asleep. She'd wanted to see him in daylight and reward him with carrots for being so good and carrying her out of danger. She spoke to Sam on the phone and heard the details of how they'd escaped from Mark's gang, who'd been arrested after the fair-haired man gave the police their names.

'You live an exciting life,' said Sam when Kiri thanked him. 'Call me again any time.'

Foxy nuzzled the girl's neck. He knew she was upset and, although he didn't understand the reason, he wanted to comfort her, just as she had comforted him when he was unhappy. He blew gently through his nostrils on to her skin, and made a soft whickering sound deep inside his throat. The hands clinging to his mane relaxed their grip.

Chapter 27

The nights were the worst time. During the day, Kiri kept herself busy enough to hold the terror of Sun Dancer's rescue at bay. But every night, she woke sweating with fear, as the violent sounds and images of that chase replayed inside her head. But the biggest competition of her life was only ten days away, so there was no choice: she had to shut out the memories and focus on her riding.

The sheer joy of being with Foxy got her through. Every time she arrived at the stables and heard him snicker with pleasure to see her she felt a warm glow inside. He might not be hers, but no one could deny the bond between them.

With Jen's help she put the finishing touches to Foxy's training, and then suddenly they were on their way to the championship at Uffington. As the horsebox finally reached the green slopes of the Lambourn

Downs, Kiri shook her head and laughed.

'I feel as if I'm in a dream. I can't believe I'm really doing this!'

Jen smiled. 'It's definitely real. And you earned it!'

With the horses settled in their stables, Mrs Jackson called a team meeting.

'I've put you in order for the dressage and cross-country according to your individual strengths. Sam will go first for our team. He'll be the pathfinder because he and Bramble are bold and reliable on the cross-country. Kiri and William will go at the end, so they can go for individual medals if we already have four good clears counting for the team score. Sarah, Viv and the rest of you will form the backbone of the team, in the middle.'

Sarah frowned and Kiri guessed she was miffed at not being selected to go at the end and given the chance of an individual medal.

The next day Kiri woke with a storm of butterflies in her stomach. She tried to cover up her nervousness by joking with Viv and Sam over breakfast.

'No bacon and eggs for you today, Sam? I thought pathfinders were never nervous.'

'Perhaps he's decided to lose weight,' mocked Viv, tipping her head on one side to consider Sam's lean build and well-muscled arms.

Sam grinned at them both. 'You can't fool me. I

know we're all feeling the same. But we've got to eat something.' He shared out a bag of croissants – something Kiri usually loved – but she struggled to force hers down.

Foxy wasn't fooled either. The tension in Kiri's hands fired him up and he started whinnying loudly. Then he arched his neck and grew taller. He was going to beat them all.

First was the dressage. It was raining, and Kiri rode into the arena with her coat soaked and her jodhpurs stuck to the saddle, but it didn't matter. Foxy was responding to her riding in a way that showed off his power and paces. She felt him float under her as they trotted circles so accurate they could have been drawn by a compass, and his canter was perfect. She was on a rising tide of elation when the sound of the judge's buzzer shocked her. She pulled Foxy up, horrified. What had gone wrong?

The judge was calling her over. 'You missed the second canter circle at B.' She gave an encouraging smile. 'Go back and start again from just before that movement.'

Kiri's face flushed and her brain went blank. How could she have made such a stupid mistake? Picking up the reins, she tried to recover the mood of the first part of their test, but she was just going through the motions, desperate to avoid a second mistake. As she came out of the arena, William gave her a pitying look but Jen was more reassuring. 'You'll lose two marks for the error, but you did so well at the beginning that the result won't be too bad.'

When at last the dressage marks for all eighty competitors were up, Kiri and Viv found themselves about a third of the way down. Sam was way below them, but William had got the best ever out of Stan to come fifth.

'Well done, everyone,' said Mrs Jackson. 'Now you must get a good night's sleep to be ready for tomorrow's cross-country.'

Kiri woke up on day two surprised that she'd been able to sleep at all. The cross-country was her best phase and everything depended on it.

'I promise not to let you down, Foxy,' she whispered, as she left his stable to go for a final course walk with Mrs Jackson and the rest of the team.

There were two kinds of fence she had never seen before.

One was a bullfinch – a metre high hedge with another metre of thin brush protruding out of the top. Mrs Jackson said to ride at it strongly and be ready for a huge leap, in case Foxy thought he had to jump over the top part of the brush instead of through it.

The other jump Kiri had never done before was the coffin.

'What a gross name for a jump!' said Viv as the team stared into the coffin-shaped ditch. First, there was an upright rail on the top of a bank, two steep strides down to the coffin followed by two strides uphill to another big rail.

'I've ridden this kind of thing often,' said William with a shrug. 'It's not as bad as it looks.'

'This is the hardest fence here,' said Mrs Jackson, giving him a sharp look. She advised them to approach the coffin slowly to give their horses time to see what they had to do.

Now it was time for the real thing, and Kiri was waiting with Sam at the start box. He was breathing fast and biting his lip.

'I don't want to let you down,' he said, gripping the reins so tightly that Bramble tossed his head.

'You won't, Sam,' said Kiri. 'You and Bramble are born to be pathfinders.'

Before she could say anything else, an official beckoned Sam into the start box and began the countdown.

'Sam Paxman, the first to go for the South East, clear over the first three fences . . . climbing the hill to number six . . . took a flier at seven but they're all right . . .'

Kiri clenched her fists as she listened to Sam's progress.

'Sam Paxman safely over number thirteen . . . now approaching the coffin . . . and yes! . . . he's taking the direct route . . .'

Kiri's nails were digging into the palms of her hands.

'. . . Bramble is slowing . . . an old-fashioned kick from Sam . . . they're over the rail . . . cat-jumped the ditch . . . but they're safely through.'

Kiri gave a whoop of excitement. When Bramble came into view, he was still galloping well. She watched him take the difficult route into the water before going out of sight again. She got to the end of the course just as Sam galloped though the finish and jumped off.

'Bramble was brilliant!'

'I knew you could do it!' Kiri thumped Sam on the back and kept Bramble walking while Sam took off the saddle, and Viv splashed water over his steaming flanks.

'That was awesome,' Sam said, still out of breath.

The whole team was exultant when the announcer said Sam was the first person to go clear without any time faults. A lot of riders were coming to grief at the coffin and Mrs Jackson decided that team policy would be to take the easier but longer route – at least until there were another three riders clear for the South East.

William and Kiri weren't due to ride until late in the afternoon. It would have been a nail-biting wait if there hadn't been so much to do helping the others. Charlotte had a stop at the water and cried her eyes out with disappointment, while Ellie and Danny both went clear but with slow times.

Kiri heard Sarah complaining to William at the start.

'They should have let me go last so I could take all the difficult options.'

'You can do that anyway,' said William. 'Just ignore team policy.'

'And spoil everyone's chances,' thought Kiri, but she didn't say anything.

She went to watch Sarah at the coffin and gasped when she saw how fast her horse, Blantyre, was approaching. They smashed into the first rail and Blantyre somersaulted, throwing Sarah into the ditch. Although Kiri rushed to help, the paramedics got there before her. She watched, chewing her nails, for a few minutes, and then breathed a sigh of relief as Sarah got shakily to her feet. Blantyre was all in one piece too.

When they got back to the stables, Mrs Jackson said nothing about team orders, but Kiri thought she didn't need to. Sarah had been given a painful lesson about listening to expert advice. Things were looking bleak for the team until Viv got round with a lot of time penalties but no jumping faults.

'We've got four team members home clear,' said

Marianne. 'That means Kiri and William can make whatever choices are best for themselves and their horses.'

Sam helped Kiri get Foxy ready, strapping protective boots over his tendons and braiding his mane so that it wouldn't fly in her face. Her legs were trembling as she pulled on her boots and she could hardly stand when her supporters arrived to wish her luck.

Kiri felt a rush of emotion as she saw them all. Marina had brought Aggie, Roxana and Ben. Roxana rushed up and gave Kiri a hug, and Ben danced around their legs. Her father had driven down from the north and – the big surprise – had picked up Steph at the airport on the way.

'Darling,' said Steph. 'When I heard you were riding in a championship, I had to be here to watch. I've brought you these.' She handed over a cross-country outfit – a sweatshirt, back protector and helmet cover, in matching shades of jade.

Kiri couldn't speak for a moment. Then she threw her arms round Steph. 'Thank you so much. You've been so kind . . .'

Steph hugged her back, and over her shoulder Kiri saw her father smiling broadly.

'Come on, my girl, aren't you going to try them on?'

'You look wonderful,' said Roxana, as she helped

Kiri put the kit on. 'Jade is definitely your colour.' She gave Kiri a silver charm in the shape of a horse's head to put in her pocket. 'That's from my great-grandma to bring you luck.' She leant forward and whispered in her ear, 'I think Mark was what she "saw" in the future. She's so grateful that you kept our family out of it that she's doing everything she can to bring you luck.'

Almost before she knew it, Kiri found herself at the start. Foxy had caught the emotions of everyone around him and was dancing round in circles.

He wanted to go NOW. Fly like the wind. Gallop and jump. Feeling her light hands on the reins, he knew that together they could do anything.

'Have fun!' said Jen.

'Go for it,' said Sam.

And she was off.

Foxy felt like a high-speed train over the first three jumps, and she had to steady him for an upright rail. Next came the bullfinch and she urged him towards what looked like an impossible two-metre barrier. She willed him to take off and he made an enormous leap that would have left her behind, if she hadn't grabbed a handful of braid. He landed safely and stormed up the scarp of the Downs, taking everything in his stride.

When they got to the top, Kiri caught a glimpse of

Uffington's famous white horse etched into the chalk.

'That's us,' she told Foxy, 'galloping together for ever.'

She steered him back down the hill, and although he pecked on landing after the drop, she stayed in the saddle. Passing another minute marker, she glanced at her stopwatch. Spot on.

Approaching the coffin, there was no question of which route to take. Horse and rider were on fire. They could jump anything. She tugged on the reins until Foxy came back to a controlled canter, which gave him time to assess the problem. He jumped the first rail neat as a cat, skipped over the ditch and bounded over the final element. Now for the water. Foxy's ears pricked and they sailed over a big log into the stream. Another look at her watch. She kicked on and he responded with a surge that felt like a river of fire carrying her through to the finish.

'Well done!' said Jen as Kiri brought Foxy to a halt. She dropped the reins and threw her arms round his sweat-soaked neck.

'No time faults – congratulations!' said Sam, checking his watch. He took the reins and looked at Kiri in surprise. 'Are you OK?'

Kiri's eyes were shining and she wiped away tears. 'It's just that he was so wonderful. Weren't you, Foxy?'

* * *

The next morning, Mrs Jackson called the team together. 'You've done very well,' she told them. 'After yesterday, our team is lying second. As individuals, Kiri is in second place after a storming cross-country while William's excellent dressage has kept him in the lead, in spite of a few time faults.'

She called for cool heads in the showjumping where the order changed so that those in the lead went last. That made it more exciting for the spectators but put a lot of pressure on the riders. When Kiri overheard William's father telling him his allowance would be cut if he didn't win, she felt a wave of warmth towards her own father.

'Have fun,' he'd said. 'I hope you win, but it doesn't matter if you don't. Not to me. Nothing matters to me except you.'

Sam, who'd already jumped a clear, wished her luck before she went into the arena. 'Don't worry,' he said. 'We're all behind you.'

But Kiri did worry. She knew how much it would mean to him and the others to get a medal, and she and William would have to do well if their team was to stay in second place.

As Kiri entered the ring, her nerves were getting worse. The team's hopes, Jen's reputation and Foxy's future were winding her up like a spring.

Kiri knew that if she couldn't keep the lid on their

shared emotions, Foxy would run amok and knock everything down. For his sake, she blanked out the crowd and rode as if she was jumping at home. She felt him relax under her and his ears locked on to the first line of fences. They were big. She cleared the first four jumps easily before checking his stride as they approached the double. Perfect. They rattled the planks and she almost forgot to breathe as she waited for the sound of one of them falling. It didn't. Round the corner to a big wall and the final stretch. Foxy flew down the line of jumps and soared over the last. The surge of applause told her she'd done it. Jumped a double clear – cross-country and showjumping!

Kiri couldn't bear to watch William's round. She would never wish bad luck on anyone, but if he made a mistake, Foxy would win and earn himself a golden future. That was the most important thing in the world. Although she clamped her hands over her ears to shut out the sounds of the crowd, she could still hear the gasps as poles were rattled but didn't fall. And then the groans as William crashed through the last two jumps.

Sam was hugging her and shouting. 'You've won! You're the champion!'

'This is the champion,' said Kiri, kissing Foxy's nose and patting his neck over and over again.

Then Jen and Viv were hugging her, and Mrs Jackson was beaming with pleasure. And when she looked up at the grandstand, Kiri could just make out her father and Steph, Roxana and her mother, and Aggie, all waving and clapping like mad.

The whole South East team came into the arena to receive silver medals. Then came the individual presentations. Sam was thrilled to get a seventh place rosette and William had dropped to fourth so Kiri was the only team member to get an individual medal.

The gold.

As she made her victory circuit of the arena, the tears came. The crowd would think they were tears of joy at winning. Only Kiri knew that her heart was being ripped out of her because this was her last ride ever on Foxy.

Half blinded, she made for the exit, but was pulled up by the ring steward, who told her to go back to the podium.

'They'll explain why when you get there.'

Uncomprehending, she returned to the podium where an official smiled at her and asked her to halt and wait. The boom of the loudspeaker filled the arena.

'Ladies and gentlemen, I have an important announcement. Most of you will know that Sun Dancer, the Derby hopeful who was kidnapped earlier this year, has been restored to his owner, Lord Haverley. What you won't know is that this world famous racehorse – worth millions of pounds – was rescued by none other than Kiri McFarlane, who minutes ago become Britain's Under Eighteen National Champion. Lord Haverley is with us now and wishes publicly to present Kiri with the reward he offered for the recovery of Sun Dancer.'

Kiri gasped as Lord Haverley stepped up to the microphone. 'Kiri McFarlane has shown the same courage and spirit here that enabled her to rescue my much-loved horse, Sun Dancer. I ask you all to applaud as I present her with a cheque in recognition of her bravery.'

The crowd cheered, flashbulbs went off and TV cameras closed in on Kiri's stunned face. The gift was generous – generous enough to let Kiri buy Foxy and bring him back to Walland Farm.

Stammering a thank you, Kiri clutched the cheque to her heart and then bent forward to clasp Foxy's warm neck with both arms. He shook his head and snorted as if to say 'I told you we could do it!'

'Another victory circuit?' suggested Lord Haverley.

Kiri picked up the reins and galloped round the arena. The crowd roared its approval but Kiri felt as if she and Foxy were alone together inside a bubble of emotion. Her heart was singing, and tears were flooding down her cheeks. Foxy, the horse she loved so much, the horse she'd nearly lost, would be hers for good.

Foxy was coming home.

* * *

Foxy tore contentedly at the herb rich grass of Walland Farm. It didn't have the lush flavour of spring but there was something about September grass that tasted good. Perhaps it was the salt, blown across the dunes by the autumn gales, or the companionship of the old pony munching at his side. Either way, Foxy was glad to be home. He swished his tail and snorted. Was she going to be late with the evening feed? No. There she was, walking across the fields with the dog at her heels and a bucket of feed swinging in her hand. As soon as she climbed over the stile into his field, he whickered to show he was pleased to see her, as well as the bucket. She scratched the special place behind his ears while he picked daintily at the feed, and when he'd finished, he rubbed his head against her shoulder. Lovely as home was, he hoped she would take him out to compete again soon. He remembered the fire in his veins as they'd galloped across country. They could never get enough of that.